Her Amish Suitor's Secret

Carrie Lighte

ISBN-13: 978-1-335-48817-6

Her Amish Suitor's Secret

This edition published by arrangement with Harlequin Books S.A.

For questions and comments about the quality of this book, please contact us at CustomerService@Harlequin.com.

Love Inspired
22 Adelaide St. West, 40th Floor
Toronto, Ontario M5H 4E3, Canada
www.Harlequin.com

Printed in U.S.A.

"Isn't it quiet where you live in Wisconsin?"

"It's not *this* quiet. This peaceful. There's something about being here, where sometimes the loudest sound I hear is water lapping the shore… It makes me feel so calm. I feel like that when I'm working in the fields, too. Probably because when I was young I used to escape to the garden when—"

"When what?" Rose pressed.

Over the past couple of weeks while chatting with Rose, Caleb had occasionally forgotten to guard his *Englisch* identity, but until now he'd always guarded his emotions, especially those concerning his upbringing. But opening up to her seemed to happen naturally. So, he continued, "My *mamm* and *daed* argued a lot and it helped to go outdoors to get away from them. Tending to *Gott*'s creation made me feel… tranquil." *Kind of like how I feel right now.*

Caleb slowly let his breath out. He dipped his paddle into the water and Rose did, too. As they journeyed he thought about how amazing it felt to confide in her. Maybe he wasn't being honest about the facts of his life, but tonight he'd been honest about his emotions.

Carrie Lighte lives in Massachusetts next door to a Mennonite farming family, and she frequently spots deer, foxes, fisher cats, coyotes and turkeys in her backyard. Having enjoyed traveling to several Amish communities in the eastern United States, she looks forward to visiting settlements in the western states and in Canada. When she's not reading, writing or researching, Carrie likes to hike, kayak, bake and play word games.

Books by Carrie Lighte

Love Inspired

Amish of Serenity Ridge

Courting the Amish Nanny
The Amish Nurse's Suitor
Her Amish Suitor's Secret

Amish Country Courtships

Amish Triplets for Christmas
Anna's Forgotten Fiancé
An Amish Holiday Wedding
Minding the Amish Baby
Her New Amish Family
Her Amish Holiday Suitor

Visit the Author Profile page at Harlequin.com.

Lay not up for yourselves treasures upon earth,
where moth and rust doth corrupt,
and where thieves break through and steal:

But lay up for yourselves treasures in heaven,
where neither moth nor rust doth corrupt, and
where thieves do not break through nor steal:

For where your treasure is,
there will your heart be also.
—*Matthew* 6:19–21

For my nieces—my youngest readers—
and in loving memory of my great-aunt Marce.

Chapter One

"You want me to pretend I'm Amish?" Caleb Miller repeated in a hushed whisper. He'd come from Madison, Wisconsin, to the Chicago suburbs to visit his brother, Ryan, and six-year-old nephew, Liam, who was asleep in the next room. "I can't do that."

"Why not? You loved living on that Amish farm when you were in college," his brother reminded him.

Caleb recalled the experience fondly. As a college student, he was a German language major with a minor in anthropology. His professor had strong ties to the Amish community, and for three summers in a row, Caleb had lived with an Amish family on a soybean farm in Pennsylvania, not far from where he went to school. "That was ten years ago. I've probably forgotten almost all of the *Deitsch* I learned," he protested.

"C'mon, you're a German language professor! You'll pick it up again in no time," Ryan countered. "You'll blend right in."

"I'm an *adjunct* faculty member. And I'm not concerned about blending in. I'm concerned about being deceptive. What you're suggesting is unethical. It wouldn't be fair to the Amish community. Posing as someone I'm not is… It's fraud. I could lose my job!"

"Tell me about it," Ryan muttered, closing his eyes and pressing his fingertips to his temples. In mid-May Caleb's brother had been suspended from his position as an archivist at the city museum after an inventory audit revealed nearly a million dollars of rare coins was missing. Two other employees had access to the collection, but the card reader indicated only Ryan had opened the storage area since the previous audit. That was almost a month ago and Ryan was losing hope of ever being reinstated. His eyes watered as he dropped his hands and looked squarely at Caleb. "I appreciate there's a risk—a very small risk—that if you do this and the university finds out, you could lose your job. But if I go to prison, there's a very high probability I'll lose my *son*."

Caleb winced at the thought. After a lengthy separation, Ryan's wife, Sheryl, had recently filed for divorce. She often held the threat of petitioning for sole custody of Liam over Ryan's head. Ryan was an excellent father, so there had been virtually no chance of the court agreeing to the request. But once the FBI investigated him and his standing at work was jeopardized, Ryan began to worry his parental rights were on shaky ground, too. He told Caleb his fear of being incarcerated was secondary compared to his fear of losing Liam. The possibility was agonizing Caleb, too, since he was crazy about his nephew, who was probably the closest Caleb would ever come to having a child of his own.

His resolve wavering, he argued feebly, "The FBI said they found no evidence of the coins at the cabins.

No evidence anyone connected to the crime had been there, either."

The first week in June, Ryan received in the mail a flyer from a small Amish lakeside camp in Serenity Ridge, Maine. The sender had circled a line of text reading: "If you can't find what you're looking for within walking or canoeing distance of your cabin, it isn't worth finding."

At first Ryan thought the anonymous message was nothing more than a marketing campaign or a hint from a colleague that he needed to take a vacation. But on the other side of the flyer someone had scrawled "Matthew 6:19–21." Ryan was familiar with the Bible verse reference, which said, "Lay not up for yourselves treasures upon earth, where moth and rust doth corrupt, and where thieves break through and steal: But lay up for yourselves treasures in heaven, where neither moth nor rust doth corrupt, and where thieves do not break through nor steal: For where your treasure is, there will your heart be also."

Ryan deduced the message was related to the stolen artifacts and he turned the note over to the FBI, who thoroughly searched the cabins and the property. Agents also interviewed the camp's owners, who were reluctant to get involved, not solely because they were Amish but also because the law enforcement's presence on-site was disruptive to their business. The FBI was equally frustrated with their record-keeping process, which amounted to little more than taking reservations by cell phone and writing the customers' last names and dates in a notebook. Furthermore, because they were Amish, the owners only accepted cash, check or money orders from their guests, which meant several of their customers were practically untraceable.

In the end, the FBI found no credible evidence to suggest the coin theft from the museum was linked to the Amish camp or its guests. The agents proposed someone with a grudge against Ryan or someone who wanted to send the FBI on a wild-goose chase had deliberately provided the false tip. They also questioned whether Ryan had convinced someone to forge the note and mail it from Maine. The suggestion was outrageous—it meant Ryan still wasn't above suspicion and left him feeling depressed.

"Just because they didn't find any evidence doesn't mean it's not there," Ryan insisted. "The detective I hired said it was possible the thief changed his mind. Maybe he heard about the FBI's investigation and figured selling the coins would be too risky."

"If that was true, wouldn't he have simply abandoned them? Why send a note hinting they're hidden near the camp in Maine?"

"The Bible verse makes me think he had a guilty conscience. The Amish don't typically evangelize, but you've said the way they put their faith into practice can be inspiring. Perhaps something the camp owners said or did made him decide he couldn't keep stolen property."

"Then why wouldn't he tell you exactly where the coins were hidden? Why just give you a vague clue?"

"I don't know. Maybe he was buying time so he could get to Canada first. Maybe another note is coming—"

Caleb interjected, "You sound a little crazy right now, Ryan."

"I *am* a little crazy right now. I can't think. I can't

sleep or eat. I'd go to Maine myself if I wasn't prohibited from leaving the area while the investigation is ongoing. And I can't afford the detective I hired any longer—I'm supporting two households as it is. If I end up being arrested, I'll need every penny I have for a decent lawyer." Ryan's pallid face contorted into a grimace. "Please, Caleb. I need your help."

"Couldn't I just stay at the cabins as a guest?"

"I already called and they said they're booked for the season. That's how I found out they need a handyman—the lady made a joke about hoping I was calling about the advertisement in *The Budget* for a resident groundskeeper. Don't you see? The timing is providential. It *has* to be."

Caleb grunted. He wasn't so sure about that. Although he'd been a Christian since he was a young boy, lately his relationship with God amounted to little more than attending church on Sunday and saying grace before a meal, if he remembered. But whether it was God's will for him to go to Maine or not, one thing Caleb did know for certain: his brother needed him. His *nephew* needed him. They were the only family he had and he couldn't let them down. "I might as well go. It's not like I'm doing anything else this summer," he said wryly.

At thirty-one, Caleb had already declared himself a confirmed bachelor. When the academic year ended each spring, he spent more time cultivating his vegetable garden than he spent cultivating personal relationships, especially with women. Having grown up in a home where his parents bickered from sunrise to sunset—eventually divorcing when Caleb was in his senior year of college—he had no desire to marry. Sure, he'd had several short-term relationships over the years, but the minute a conflict arose, Caleb broke up with the woman. He'd rather be lonely than wind up as miserable as his parents had been. Or as his brother was now.

"Are you being serious?" Ryan asked.

"Yeah, I'll go."

"Woo-hoo!" Ryan yelped, and practically crushed Caleb's shoulders in a bear hug until Liam padded into the room.

"What's wrong, Daddy?" he asked, bleary-eyed.

"Nothing, son. I was shouting because Uncle Caleb told me good news. He's going away this summer. On a nice long vacation."

"You are? But you just got here." Liam looked as if he was about to cry. He'd become very clingy since Ryan moved into an apartment and saw him only on the weekends. "Can we come, too?"

Caleb winced at his plea. "It's not going to be a real vacation, Liam. I'll be working. I'll tell you what—next time I come back, you and I can go camping together. How's that?"

Liam nodded slowly. "Okay. But when will you get back?"

"Soon," Caleb promised. "Just as soon as I can."

"I hope everything goes smoothly for you and the girls while we're away," Rose Allgyer's aunt Nancy said at the end of Rose's second week helping run Serenity Lake Cabins.

"I've owned and managed a restaurant in one of the busiest tourist areas in Lancaster County, so don't worry about us," Rose said. "You've got enough on your mind." Rose's aunt and uncle were traveling from Maine to Ohio to participate in an eight- to ten-week clinical trial for patients with renal cell cancer and wouldn't return home until the last week in August.

"*Gott* willing, this treatment will be exactly what Sol needs." Nancy angled her face toward the lake. It was the third week in June and the temperatures were already in the mideighties, but a cool breeze stirred the water and drifted up the hill to where they were relaxing on the porch. "It will be so *gut* to see my *schweschder* and her *familye* in Ohio again. It's been almost ten years since we moved away. I love it here, but I do miss everybody back home."

A couple of years after relocating from Ohio to a new Amish settlement in Serenity Ridge, Maine, Nancy and Sol had purchased the Maine camp. They earned their living by selling produce and renting the cabins to fishermen, young families, older couples and artists and writers who enjoyed solitude and simplicity. *And* good cooking—Nancy and her sixteen-year-old twin daughters, Charity and Hope, along with one other staff member, served a full breakfast and supper and a light lunch in the main dining hall every day except Sunday.

As Rose had discovered during the past two weeks, harvesting produce and cooking for that many people, as well as cleaning the cabins and washing linens on Saturdays, was hard work. But, as she told her aunt, the guests here were generally less demanding than the *Englischers* she encountered at the restaurant in Pennsylvania.

"*Jah*, our guests are very respectful of the property and each other's privacy. Many of them have been coming here every year since we opened. That's why I regretted the tumult I told you about with the FBI at the start of the season. It was so disruptive to all of us. You can't imagine how intrusive some of the agents' questions were. And they went through our record keeping with a fine-tooth comb."

If only I'd gone through my *business records with a fine-tooth comb, perhaps I wouldn't be broke right now,* Rose thought bitterly. Earlier that spring she'd discovered her fiancé, Baker Zook, had been taking money from the restaurant she owned. The small eatery originally belonged to Baker's mother, but when she passed away two years ago, Rose became the new proprietor. Baker, a horse trainer by trade, had been handling the accounting successfully until that time, and Rose saw no reason to hire anyone else once she took over the business. During the course of the following year, her professional relationship with Baker developed into a romantic courtship and the pair had planned to get married in the upcoming autumn wedding season.

That was before she learned Baker had been skimming money from the restaurant's account to buy and resell racehorses. He admitted his wrongdoing only when one of the most expensive horses he'd invested in strained its suspensory ligament, rendering it incapable of competing. Unable to hide the financial loss, Baker confessed to the church leaders and apologized to Rose. The deacons had helped him devise a bimonthly repayment schedule, but it would be another two years before Rose would be fully recompensed. Meanwhile, she had defaulted on a business loan and had to forfeit the lease on her restaurant.

The irony is that I was drawn to Baker because, unlike any suitor I ever had, he seemed to respect that I was an independent business owner. In retrospect Rose realized Baker probably only valued her professional success because it funded his equine wheeling and dealing. She felt utterly humiliated she'd been bamboozled, and her embarrassment was compounded by her family, who hadn't wanted her to buy the restaurant in the first place.

"If you had gotten married when you were young like your sisters did, you wouldn't be in this predicament now," her mother had lectured. "You're twenty-nine, and you have no husband and no income. Who is going to provide for you once *Daed* and I are gone?"

Trying to convince her family she'd been better off without a man in her life and that she could take care of herself was futile, so she decided she'd have to *show* them instead. Rose set her sights on leasing a small café when she returned to Pennsylvania at the end of the summer. However, even though the salary her aunt and uncle were paying her was generous, it still wasn't enough for her to be able to afford the initial rent and deposit for the new location.

"Would you and *Onkel* Sol mind if I come up with a way to bring in extra income on my own time while I'm here?" she asked Nancy. As a business owner herself, Rose's aunt had been one of the few people who had supported Rose's endeavors with the restaurant.

"Of course not, as long as it doesn't hinder your service to our guests or disrupt their privacy. And don't wear yourself too thin. Charity and Hope are *gut* workers, but as you've probably noticed, Eleanor sometimes talks quicker than she works," Nancy warned.

Rose chuckled. She *had* noticed that Eleanor Sutter, the twenty-one-year-old woman who came in the late afternoon to help prepare and serve supper, was a real chatterbox.

"Once Caleb Miller arrives, he'll take over the upkeep of the fields and the two of you can work together on harvesting the produce. Sol usually manages the finances, but I'd rather not assign that to Caleb, since we don't know much about him, except he said he's a distant *gschwischderkind* of the Miller *familye* in Blue Hill, Ohio, where I grew up. And any relative of theirs is a friend of mine. Do you feel confident handling the accounting?"

"Absolutely!" Rose declared. *There's no way I'm going to make the mistake of delegating that responsibility to someone else again.* As it was, after Rose learned the camp's usual caretaker had broken his leg, she had tried to convince Nancy and Sol it wasn't necessary for them to hire a resident replacement. Rose suggested they could save money by employing an hourly worker to make any urgent repairs the cabins needed, and she insisted she and the twins could manage the gardens on their own. But her aunt was resolute, claiming so much had been left undone because of Sol's illness she didn't want the camp's condition to deteriorate further. Also, Hope and Charity both served as nannies for local Amish mothers from after breakfast until almost supper on weekdays, which meant they wouldn't be available to pitch in during the day.

Rose sipped her lemonade and then asked, "When is Caleb arriving anyway?"

"Tomorrow afternoon around four o'clock."

Rose frowned. "It's odd that he'd travel on the *Sabbat*, don't you think?"

"*Neh*, not especially. We travel when we visit our friends after church on *Suundaag*."

"*Jah*, but you don't pay someone to transport you—

you take your own buggy. Isn't hiring an *Englisch* driver or taking the train kind of like conducting business or going shopping?"

"The bishop allows it, so..." Nancy said with a shrug. Then she gently added, "I know Baker broke your heart, Rose—"

"He didn't break my heart. He broke my trust," Rose cut in. She would *not* give Baker credit for breaking her heart, even if that was exactly what he'd done.

"*Jah*, he definitely broke your trust," Nancy acknowledged. "But not every young man you meet is going to be as unscrupulous as he was. I hope you'll give Caleb a chance to demonstrate what kind of person he is before you come to any conclusions about his character."

"Of course, I will," Rose assured her aunt. *Although, I can't imagine spending much time getting to know him.*

"*Gut.* Working together will be a lot easier if you do. And maybe the two of you will wind up becoming friends," Nancy suggested.

I need to make money, not friends, Rose thought, biting her lip. But when she noticed her aunt scrutinizing her, she smiled and said, "Who knows, maybe we will."

After the van driver dropped him off at the end of the long dirt driveway—which appeared more like a road—leading to the lakeside cabins, Caleb inhaled the piney scent, trying to calm his nerves. He'd spent nearly every moment since he called Nancy the weekend before preparing for his arrival here. He'd ordered an Amish hat and clothing and listened to as many recordings of people speaking *Deitsch* as he could find online. He'd even considered traveling thc hour and a half from Madison to Green Lake County to hang out at the Amish market and practice the language, but he didn't want to do anything to draw attention to himself.

He surveyed the fields as he ambled past them. Nancy had told him most of the acreage was used for berries and potatoes, but they also grew a variety of fruits and vegetables, from asparagus to watermelons and everything in between. From what Caleb could discern, their crops were flourishing. He'd developed an interest in horticulture as a teenager, when being alone outdoors provided him with an escape from his parents' quarrels, and Caleb anticipated managing the gardens would be the most pleasant part of his role here, too.

The open fields gave way to a little forest of pine trees and once he'd trekked another quarter of a mile, Caleb spied what appeared to be the main house, as well as the roofs and back walls of several small cabins. He dallied a moment in the shade, his heart thumping in his ears. He felt as nervous as if he were waiting offstage, about to perform in a play—and in a way, he was.

"Wilkom," a trim middle-aged woman called from the porch of the main house as Caleb approached. She pushed herself up from the wooden glider and waved to him.

"Guder nammidaag," he replied, his voice cracking dryly.

"I'm Nancy Petersheim," she said when he climbed the steps. "You must be Caleb Miller."

"I am, *jah*," he answered awkwardly, and set down his suitcase. Some Amish shook hands and others didn't, so he waited for Nancy to take the lead.

"You walked in from the road? You must be parched.

I'll bring you a cool drink and a slice of Rose's *aebeer babrag boi*. Take a seat."

Caleb knew *aebeer* meant *strawberry* and *boi* meant *pie*, but his mind went blank on the word *babrag*. He sat in a glider and scanned the grounds. The property in front of the main house sloped down toward the lake. From where he was situated on the porch, Caleb's view of the water was partially obscured by trees, but he could see enough of the lake to understand why it was referred to as *pristine* on the flyer his brother had received. He counted nine small cabins tucked beneath the pines, each one angled toward the water. To his delight, he noticed the ground was covered in needles. *No grass means no mowing.* His least favorite part of yard work.

He turned toward the door as Nancy emerged with a tray of goodies. *That's right.* Babrag *means* rhubarb. Caleb hadn't realized how hungry he was until he took a bite of strawberry-rhubarb pie, the perfect marriage of tart and sweet. He briefly closed his eyes as he savored the flavor, amazed he'd forgotten how scrumptious Amish food could be.

"*Appenditlich*, isn't it?" Nancy beamed. "My niece, Rose, makes the best *boi* I've ever tasted. She's the one who will be doing most of the cooking while we're away."

"Jah, appenditlich," he agreed, shoveling a large forkful into his mouth. Caleb figured by keeping his mouth full he could avoid answering questions until his nerves steadied. Fortunately, as he was finishing the dessert, Nancy cocked an ear toward the screen door.

"I hear my husband, Sol, stirring. When he first gets up from a nap, he's a little woozy. You'll get to meet him at supper. For now, why don't you familiarize yourself with the grounds and make yourself at home in your cabin?" She pointed toward a tiny structure on the water's edge. "You'll be staying in that one, cabin number nine. Actually, we sometimes call it cabin eight and a half because it's so small, but it has the best location."

Caleb meandered happily down the path, relieved his initial interaction with Nancy had gone off without a hitch. *Maybe this won't be as difficult as I imagined*, he hoped. Of course, convincing his employer he was Amish was a minor accomplishment compared to finding the evidence his brother needed him to find. But at least he'd made it over the first hurdle.

The humidity caused the cabin door to stick in its frame, and Caleb had to nudge it open with his shoulder. Once inside, he found the one-room structure contained a single bed, an armchair, a desk-and-chair set, a bureau and a gas lamp. There was a separate stall with a toilet, sink and shower. *I guess this is what the flyer meant by simply furnished*, he thought. But the view through the picture window more than made up for the scarcity of furnishings: not ten yards away Serenity Lake sparkled with sunlight, and in the distance, hills abundant with verdant trees encircled the shoreline.

After a little experimenting Caleb figured out the picture window opened perpendicularly instead of horizontally. He swung it toward himself on its hinge and then fastened the bottom sill with hooks to the beams overhead. Within seconds a soft breeze wafted across his face and he closed his eyes to relish the sensation. *I'd better keep moving or I'm likely to doze off and miss supper*, he thought, so he began unpacking his suitcase.

It didn't take long. Aside from a couple changes of clothes and toiletries, all Caleb had brought with him was his cell phone and a solar-powered charger.

He and Ryan had agreed that for the duration of his stay Caleb would call his brother only on Saturdays. Caleb would have to keep the phone muted, although they'd text or leave messages with each other about any urgent developments. Caleb stashed the phone in the middle drawer before removing his final possession from the side pocket of the suitcase: a photo of Liam, grinning broadly to show he'd lost a front tooth. On the back of the photo he'd written "I love you!" Caleb smiled before sliding the picture into a Bible he'd found in the top drawer of the bureau.

Stepping outside, he noticed the camp was unusually quiet, not a guest in sight. Maybe they were out fishing? As he walked toward the narrow stretch of sand in front of the dock, he noticed a sign that read No Swimming or Sunbathing. Doubtless, the Amish owners found *Englisch* swimwear too immodest to allow guests to wear it while on their property. However, according to the flyer the camp did provide two canoes and two rowboats for their guests' use, as well as a shed full of fishing gear they could borrow. *I wouldn't mind vacationing at a place like this myself,* Caleb thought. *Too bad Liam couldn't come here with me.*

He'd been so nervous anticipating his meeting with Nancy and Sol, he hadn't noticed until just then how much his feet ached. He hadn't gotten a chance to break in the new work boots he'd bought before he left Wisconsin, and he was sure he had blisters on his heels. As he bent to unlace the boots so he could dip his feet in the water, he spotted a flash of color from the corner of his eye. A woman wearing a cobalt blue dress was paddling a canoe around a large rock that jutted into the water some two hundred yards down the shoreline.

That must be Rose, he thought as she drew closer. She looked too mature to be one of the sixteen-year-old daughters Nancy had told him about on the phone. The woman's strokes were smooth and sure, and in no time she'd bypassed the dock, apparently preferring to disembark on the shore. Deeply tanned, she had a kerchief instead of a prayer *kapp* fastened over her dark hair, and her forehead glistened with perspiration. Her face was all broad planes and sharp angles and if Caleb didn't know she was Amish, he would have claimed for certain she was wearing rose-red lipstick—was that how she'd gotten her name?

"Don't just stand there—move!" she hollered as she propelled the fore end of the canoe onto the shore, nearly bowling into him. He jumped back just in time.

No, Caleb decided. *Her parents probably named her Rose because they knew how prickly she'd be.*

As Rose got out of the canoe, the man greeted her. "*Guder nammidaag.* I'm Caleb. Caleb Miller. You must be Rose."

"Jah," she answered tersely, pulling the canoe farther onto shore. *We haven't even started working together and he's already getting in my way.* She knew she should welcome him or say she was glad he'd arrived, but she didn't appreciate the way he'd been gawking at her. The most she could ask by way of hospitality was, "How was your trip?"

"Gut, denki," he answered as he helped her flip the canoe over in the sand. His dark curly hair poked out from beneath his hat, and when he looked at her she noticed he had the longest eyelashes she'd ever seen on a man; they made his blue eyes appear all the more

luminous. Or was that a trick of the light off the lake? "How was yours?"

"My what?" Rose was annoyed at herself for being flustered by him. Gut-*looking doesn't mean* gut *acting*, she thought, remembering her sisters frequently commenting about how handsome Baker was.

"Your canoeing trip." He pointed toward the water.

"Oh, it was fine." It hadn't been fine. It was hot and buggy, and the only reason she'd stayed out all afternoon was because she didn't want to be at the house while Eleanor's twenty-four-year-old brother, Henry, tried to flirt with her under the guise of visiting Nancy and Sol. Rose unfastened her life vest and hung it in the shed nearby.

When she emerged, Caleb handed her her sneakers and grinned. Wisconsin must have something special in their water, she thought—his teeth were as white as the *Englisch* celebrities on the covers of magazines at the superstore. The clanking of a bell interrupted Rose's thoughts. "That's *Ant* Nancy's signal supper is ready."

Although she was still barefoot, Rose trod easily on the path up the hill, with Caleb lagging behind. *I hope he doesn't* always *move as slowly as what I've seen so far.* There was a bin of water and a towel outside the door on the porch. Rose dunked one foot into the bin and then the other, rinsing them free of pine needles and then drying them before going inside with Caleb.

"Ah, I see you two have met, Caleb and Rose," Nancy said. She introduced her husband to Caleb and explained Hope and Charity had gone to a singing that evening and wouldn't be joining them for supper. Then everyone took a seat at the kitchen table.

"I'll say grace," Sol announced, giving Caleb a moment to remove his hat.

Don't they have any manners in Wisconsin? Rose wondered when Caleb didn't take the hint.

"There's a hook near the door for your *hut* or you can hang it on your chair, Caleb," Nancy kindly suggested.

"My apologies," Caleb replied, sweeping his hat off his head and balancing it on the back of his chair. Rose noticed his face was still aflame after Sol finished praying and everyone lifted their heads again.

"What is your occupation in Wisconsin that allows you to come all the way to Maine at this time of year?" she asked.

"I'm a teacher."

Rose cocked her head, intrigued. "I've heard some settlements are so small they have male teachers instead of female teachers, but I've never spoken to one. What's your favorite part of working with *scholars*?"

"I, uh, enjoy teaching *Deutsche*," Caleb said, taking an enormous bite of his ham-and-cheese sandwich. When he finished chewing he addressed Sol. "Your wife told me on the phone I'd be taking care of the *gaerde* and *baamgaarde* as well as maintaining the grounds and cabins. What kind of repair projects have you been working on?"

"There will be time enough for discussing work when the *Sabbat* is over," Nancy said, and again Caleb's cheeks went red.

Like Rose, her uncle must have noticed Caleb's embarrassment, because Sol waved his hand and commented, "Nancy's just worried if you find out how much work there is to do, you'll turn around and go back to Wisconsin in the middle of the night."

That wouldn't be the worst thing in the world, Rose thought facetiously.

"I'll take you around tomorrow morning and show you everything," Sol continued. "I've made a few to-do lists, but most of your responsibilities will be typical gardening and maintenance projects. Making sure everything is functional and tidy for our guests. And keeping shifty-looking types from prowling around the property."

"Shifty-looking types?" Caleb coughed, wide-eyed. "Have you had a problem with unwelcome people on the property?"

"Perhaps not unwelcome, but uninvited, *jah.*" Sol winked at his wife before explaining to Caleb, "Our Rose hasn't even been here a month and we've already had more bachelors visiting us the past couple *Suundaage* than we've had all spring. I get the feeling once Nancy and I leave they're going to find excuses to *kumme* by during the week, too. So if you notice any young men hanging around or acting strange, feel free to tell them to scram—"

"Onkel!" Rose was sure her face was even redder than Caleb's had been. She didn't need the likes of a slow-moving, ill-mannered man like Caleb looking out for her. She didn't need *any* man looking out for her, for that matter.

"Something tells me Rose would chase away any unsavory characters long before I got to them," Caleb remarked, and she didn't know whether it was a compliment or a criticism. Either way, she didn't care.

"You've got that right. The only fishy behavior I'll put up with is from the bass and trout in Serenity Lake," she declared. Everyone cracked up, and Rose laughed along with them even though she couldn't have been more serious.

Chapter Two

Caleb woke shortly after first light. The battery-operated clock on the desk said it was only a little past four; the sun wasn't even up yet. But since he'd turned in early the night before and he'd had such a refreshing sleep, he got up and dressed anyway. Now what? He wished he'd brought something to read; the Bible was the only book in the cabin. He leafed through it until he got to the sixth chapter of Matthew so he could review verses 19–21. By now he had them practically memorized, but he still wasn't convinced they had anything to do with the stolen coins from the museum. As he flipped the page back and skimmed the chapter from the beginning, the words of the Lord's Prayer caught his eye and it occurred to him he should pray.

It had been so long since he'd spent any time in prayer he felt sheepish talking to the Lord now, but Caleb bowed his head and mumbled, "God, I know I haven't been very faithful lately, but Ryan is desperate, so if there is something here at the cabins that will help prove my brother's innocence, will You please show it to me?" Caleb meditated silently for several minutes, listening to the rhythmic slapping of water against the shore before opening his eyes and rising.

Sol had said to meet him on the porch at six o'clock, which was also when Rose or one of Sol's daughters collected eggs and milked the cow. Caleb kind of wished that would be his responsibility. He'd enjoyed milking when he lived on the Amish farm, but he was out of practice. Surely the *meed* would appreciate it if he did it for them, he thought as he headed toward the barn on the other side of the main house and then went inside. Even with the door open it took a moment for his eyes to adjust to the lack of light.

Scanning the organized interior, he glimpsed the family's milk cow and horse. The buggy and harness were also housed in the barn, as well as hay, feed and sundry farming tools and supplies. Caleb briefly considered whether the coins could have been stashed among them, but on first look he saw nothing resembling the carrying case or small safe Ryan said the thief would have been likely to use to transport the valuables. Besides, the barn was a highly trafficked area. *If I were concealing stolen goods, I'd hide them someplace that was off the beaten path. Like in the woods.* Taking a fresh pail from the hook and removing the stainless steel lid, Caleb set about milking the cow and he was surprised by how quickly the process came back to him. "Good girl," he said, patting the gentle animal when he was finished, grateful she'd been so passive.

The sun was up and the sky bright when he walked outside. Still, he doubted it was six o'clock yet and he figured he might as well gather the eggs, too. Maybe by doing a few extra chores he'd get on Rose's good side. Although he would usually avoid a young woman altogether if she seemed peevish toward him, Caleb couldn't afford to alienate anyone at the camp. Besides, he surmised maybe he shouldn't take Rose's snippy attitude personally. During supper he learned she'd been in Maine for only a couple of weeks herself; maybe when she saw him onshore she mistook him for another uninvited caller. Sol indicated she had several men vying for her affections, which must be irritating since she clearly wasn't interested in being courted.

Caleb set down the milk pail, entered the coop and unlatched the door to the henhouse. The chickens were less cooperative than the cow had been and he incurred a few pecks on his wrist and hand as he wrested a couple of broody birds from the nesting box. After successfully retrieving his first egg, he realized he didn't have a basket, so he swept his hat off his head and deposited the egg inside it. He'd collected a good dozen when he heard a woman's voice behind him.

"Exactly what do you think you're doing?" It was Rose, and she sounded every bit as thorny this morning as she had yesterday evening by the lake.

"Guder mariye," he replied congenially. "I'm collecting *oier*."

"That's *my* responsibility. Or Hope and Charity's."

"I don't mind."

"*I* do. I need every one of those to make breakfast for the guests. Your *hut* isn't sturdy enough for you to pile so many on top of each other in it—they'll break."

"Sorry." Caleb carefully supported the bottom of his hat as he extended it to Rose so she could transfer the eggs into her basket. When she'd taken the last one, he turned on his heel and hightailed it away from her.

He was halfway across the yard when she squawked,

"Hey! You didn't shut the door—the *hinkel* are getting out!"

Spinning around, Caleb saw three chickens had escaped the coop and several more were streaming out. He dashed toward them with his arms spread wide to herd them back into the coop, but his feet were still sore from the blisters so he wasn't as nimble as he needed to be. Rose came to his aid and by the time the chickens were inside again and she had secured the door behind her, she was red-faced and scowling. She picked up the egg basket and waited for him to retrieve the milk pail from where he'd left it in the grass earlier.

"Are you sure you're Amish?" she asked as they walked toward the house.

Uh-oh. "Wh-what do you mean?" he stuttered.

"My four- and five-year-old nieces and nephews know better than to leave the coop door open. They also know you should do the milking after collecting the *oier*, so you can bring the *millich* inside right away. We can't drink this now. I'll have to make *sauer millich kuche* instead."

Relieved his *Englisch* identity hadn't been found out, Caleb smiled. "If your *sauer millich kuche* is anything like your *aebeer babrag boi*, then I'm glad I didn't bring the *millich* inside right away."

Rose rolled her eyes—he noticed they were amber, not brown as he'd first thought. "Flattery will get you nowhere," she said, but a tiny smile decorated her lips. "I'm just glad you didn't leave the *corral* door open. The *gaul* is much harder to round up than the *hinkel*."

"Are you speaking from personal experience?"

Caught, she giggled. "*Jah.* I suppose you're not the

only one who's careless the first morning after a long day of travel."

Caleb laughed. "Tomorrow I'll do better, I promise." If he lasted that long without blowing his cover.

When they returned to the house, Sol was waiting on the porch to give Caleb a tour of the property and review his to-do list, which included maintaining the grounds, cabins, dock and boats, cultivating the gardens and orchards, caring for the livestock and completing a host of other minor chores, as well. How would he ever keep up with all of this and still have time to look for the coins, Caleb wondered.

When they circled back to the porch, Sol gazed down the hill toward the water. "There's a lot to be done, but be sure to have a little *schpass* while you're here," he advised. There was a catch in his voice as he added, "It's a shame there's not enough time for me to take you out on the lake to show you the best fishing spots..."

Sensing Sol was nervous about his upcoming treatment, Caleb assured him, "You can show me when you return." *If I'm still here.*

"I'll look forward to that," Sol replied, grinning again.

After the last guests departed the dining hall and while Hope and Charity were clearing their dishes, Rose prepared the family's breakfast. Usually, her aunt would have been helping, too, but on Mondays Nancy went to the bank first thing in the morning. Rose didn't mind—she liked being in charge.

Serving guests here seemed easier than at her restaurant in Pennsylvania, probably because at the camp everyone ate together, family-style, at long picnic tables. Instead of ordering individual meals, for breakfast and supper guests were offered two main entrées, homemade bread or buns, various garden fruits and vegetables, and of course, something sweet, such as doughnuts in the morning and desserts in the evening. For the noon meal, guests could make their own lunch or help themselves to the platters of bread, fruit and cheese Nancy or the girls set out for them, buffet-style. If guests had special dietary needs, they were welcome to use the kitchen to prepare their own meals either before or after the regular meal hours, but otherwise, everyone ate as much or as little as they liked from what was offered. Nancy said in the seven years since they opened the cabins to the public, she'd never received a single complaint.

Glancing through the large window-like opening in the wall that separated the kitchen from the dining area, Rose reminded Charity to set an extra place at the table for Caleb.

"*Mamm* said you met him yesterday. What's he like?" Hope asked casually, causing Rose to suppress a smile. Having just turned sixteen, the twins were allowed to court now, and Rose had observed subtle signs of flirting when they interacted with certain boys at church. She remembered being that naive and optimistic about romance. It was *gut* to enjoy it while it lasted.

"He's probably a little older than I am," she said, knowing Caleb's age would dash their hopes of having him as a suitor.

Sure enough, Hope moaned, clearly disappointed. "Aw, that's too bad."

"He's also rather *doppich*." Rose only added that he was clumsy by way of consolation.

"Doppich?" Charity echoed from the dining area. "How so?"

"Well, let's just say he's not very light on his feet. Not very quick, either," Rose replied with a laugh. "I almost ran him over with the canoe yesterday—and he was standing onshore! And this morning he let the *hinkel* out and it took him five minutes to round them up again."

"That's because my new boots are giving me blisters," Caleb clarified.

Uh-oh. When did he kumme *in and how much did he hear?* Rose was mortified she might have been caught talking about Caleb, especially in unflattering terms. "Oh, uh, that's too bad. After breakfast I'll give you a couple adhesive bandages," she offered. She ducked her head and pushed eggs around in a skillet as she listened to him introduce himself to Charity and Hope. A moment later she heard Nancy and Sol enter the dining hall, too.

As they ate, Rose noted she'd have to make more food next time: Caleb had a voracious appetite, and he hardly gave himself time to swallow in between bites of scrapple and eggs. After everyone's plate was empty, Sol reached for his wife's hand and cleared his throat, but it was Nancy who spoke.

"We want you all to know how much it means to us that we can count on you to keep the camp running smoothly. These next couple of months are going to be challenging and—" Her eyes filled and she stopped speaking.

Rose got up and walked around to the other side of the table. Squeezing in between Sol and Nancy, she gave them each a sideways hug. "It's a privilege to help and we'll be praying faithfully for you." Then she offered to finish cleaning up so Hope and Charity could accompany their parents to the house until the van arrived.

Caleb solemnly shook Sol's and Nancy's hands—such a formal gesture, but perhaps that was what the Wisconsin Amish did, Rose thought—and after they left, he gulped down a final swig of coffee and took off for the fields. It wasn't until Rose was bringing the tray of dirty dishes into the kitchen that she remembered he needed an adhesive bandage. *Oh, well, I'll give him one later.*

For now, she was reveling in the solitude. She liked being alone, even if it meant she had to do all the work by herself, because it gave her time to flesh out her plan for earning more money without neglecting her responsibilities at the camp. Since she needed to be available to the guests, she couldn't take another part-time job in town. *Too bad I couldn't open the dining hall to the public*, she thought. But that would definitely ruin the camp's tranquil, isolated atmosphere—a huge no-no in her aunt's book.

The roadside fruit-and-vegetable stand was as close as Nancy and Sol allowed the general public to come to the camp. Typically, the Petersheims sold whatever produce they didn't serve to the guests or use and can for themselves. However, so far this season they seemed to have a bumper crop of almost everything they grew, so Rose decided she'd put up the extra vegetables and use the fruit to make jam and sell it at the stand. She'd split the proceeds with her aunt and uncle, of course, since it was their harvest. *Englischers* back home were willing to pay a pretty penny for homemade jams and naturally preserved foods, and she imagined the same would be true of the *Englischers* in Maine. The extra income wouldn't be enough to secure the lease for the café, but it would be a start until Rose could devise a more lucrative plan.

In between completing the rest of her chores at the camp, she took a trip into town for jars and other supplies, and then she spent the afternoon strawberry picking so she could make a double batch of jam the following day. She was pleased with her progress but exhausted by the time Eleanor arrived and the twins returned home to help her prepare the guests' dinner.

"What's Caleb Miller like?" Eleanor asked, undoubtedly for the same reason the twins had inquired about him.

This time, Rose answered more carefully. "You'll get to meet him soon yourself."

Blithely Eleanor tugged Rose's sleeve. "Just tell me one little thing about him."

"He's in need of a bandage for a blister on his foot," Rose retorted, her patience wearing thin. "Now, chop that asparagus, please. It's already been washed."

"Is he tall?" Eleanor persisted. At five eleven, she was even taller than Rose.

"That's two things." Rose pointed to the heap of stalks on the cutting board. "The asparagus, please."

"*Jah*, he's tall," Charity told Eleanor. "But he's old."

Eleanor picked up a knife. "How old?"

"At least thirty, maybe older."

"Kind of strange he's not married yet," Hope remarked.

"Thirty's not so old to be single. Not for a man anyway." Eleanor shot Rose an exaggeratedly contrite look. "Oops, sorry, Rose."

"Don't be," she snapped. "I'm not."

After spending the day repairing the dock, grooming the livestock and cleaning their stalls, fertilizing the gardens, digging up tubers and harvesting asparagus, as well as pruning the shrubbery around the camp, Caleb's arm and back muscles were so sore he didn't give a second thought to the blisters on his feet. While his work allowed him plenty of opportunities to scope out the property, he was discouraged to discover how thick the undergrowth was in the woods on both sides of the camp. The coins could be anywhere—or nowhere.

He'd stopped moving only long enough to eat lunch in the dining hall around one thirty. By then, the guests had helped themselves to the light buffet, and two empty pie tins were the only evidence that Rose had set out pies for dessert. Caleb made a mental note to take his break earlier the following day. He suspected Rose would have baked more pies by then, as he'd crossed paths with her in the strawberry patch about a half hour ago. When he'd asked if she needed help picking berries, she waved him away. She seemed almost proprietorial about her duties, and Caleb remembered many Amish women considered their houses and gardens to be their domain. Not that Rose was like any other Amish woman he'd met, but still, Caleb figured it would be wise to give her a wide berth. After what he'd overheard her saying about him that morning he didn't want to be considered intrusive, as well as clumsy and slow.

At suppertime he felt slightly out of place as the only man among four women. To make matters more uncomfortable, Eleanor riddled him with questions about his life in Wisconsin. He tried to keep his answers as honest as he could, but his replies sounded evasive to his own ears.

"Wisconsin is so far away. Won't you miss your *familye*?" she asked.

"My *eldre* died years ago, so it's just my *bruder* and me now." Caleb didn't mention his nephew for fear it would lead to questions about Sheryl. He didn't want to slip up and mention the pending divorce, which would be a giveaway since the Amish never divorced.

"What about your friends? Or your girlfriend?"

Caught off guard because most Amish people weren't so candid in inquiring about romantic relationships, Caleb admitted, "I don't have a girlfriend, and I'll be too busy to miss anyone else."

Eleanor fluttered her lashes. "If you need my help with anything, just let me know. I've worked here every summer for the past five years, so I know this camp inside and out. If you'd like I could show you around the lake, too."

That could come in handy in his quest for the coins. "*Denki.* I might take you up on that offer."

"The guests have first dibs on the canoes and rowboats during the week," Rose quickly informed him. "*Suundaag* is the only day we're allowed to use them."

"Why? Don't the guests go fishing or canoeing on *Suundaag*?"

"Sometimes they do, but since we don't serve meals on the *Sabbat*, most of them take the opportunity to go boating on Black Bear Lake, across town. The fishing isn't nearly as *gut* but they can use motorboats there. Or they spend the day hiking or sightseeing, and shopping or dining in the area."

Caleb filed this bit of information away in his mind. Might the crook have taken advantage of the empty camp to hide the coins then? "Have you, uh, ever had any problems with unruly guests?" he ventured.

Rose tipped her head quizzically. "Why do you ask that?"

Fortunately, Eleanor was more forthcoming. "*I* have," she complained. "Hope and Charity, remember that guy who yelled at me a few weeks ago?"

"Because you tipped over his *millich*, right?"

"*Jah*. He was *narrish*. Your *daed* very politely told him that's not how we treat each other at the camp, and he stormed out of the dining hall." Eleanor snickered. "They apparently were so offended they left that night and it was only the third day of their vacation."

Caleb's pulse quickened. "They? Was he here with someone else?" *An accomplice?*

"*Jah*, he was with his wife, I think. Or maybe she was his girlfriend. You know how *Englischers* are. They think nothing of—"

"That's enough, Eleanor," Rose cut in, glancing at her nieces. "We're here to serve our guests and to be an example of *Gott*'s love, not to pry or gossip about their private lives."

Caleb's cheeks burned, but he was grateful for the information Eleanor disclosed. If he could gain access to the reservation book, maybe he could figure out which cabin the couple had stayed in. Not that they were necessarily the thieves, but it was worth noting their behavior seemed out of the ordinary. If he determined which cabin they'd rented, he could turn it inside out once Saturday rolled around.

According to Sol, Saturday was changeover day. The current guests had to depart by ten in the morning, and the new guests weren't allowed to arrive until two o'clock. Meanwhile, the girls cleaned and put fresh linens on the beds, while Caleb was expected to give the cabins a once-over, to be sure everything was in working order.

"I didn't mean to meddle," Caleb said. "I, er, just wanted to know what to expect in case you ever needed me to, uh, step in..."

"That won't be necessary." Rose's tone was as vinegary as Eleanor's was honeyed.

"Speaking of stepping in," the younger woman cooed, "Rose mentioned you needed a bandage for your foot. If you *kumme* up to the *haus* with me, I'll give you one."

"*Neh.* I'll get it," Rose sternly objected. "You stay here and wash the dishes."

Caleb loitered in the dining hall until Rose returned, as it was clear she didn't want him to accompany her, either. Too bad—going with Eleanor might have provided the perfect opportunity to sneak a peek at the reservation book, since she appeared eager to gain his favor.

By Saturday Caleb had settled into his daily routine and he'd made great strides in his use of *Deitsch*, but he was no closer to figuring out where the couple Eleanor mentioned had stayed. He gave the cabins a thorough search, which wasn't difficult since they were so small and uncluttered. Virtually identical to each other, each one consisted of an open living area with a picture window overlooking the lake, and two tiny bedrooms, as well as a compact bathroom. The furniture was exactly like his, except in addition to an armchair every cabin contained a small sofa. Caleb even examined the floors for loose boards and checked the dirt around the buildings' foundations to see if it had been overturned.

Nothing unusual jumped out at him. The only stray items he found left behind were a damp towel and a pair of sunglasses.

He regretted having nothing of importance to share with Ryan when he called him on Saturday evening at their agreed-upon time. Caleb lowered the picture window and closed the door so no one would hear him talking.

"How was your first week?" Ryan's question was casual, but his voice was tremulous.

"*Gut*—I mean good. I'm beat, though. I always prided myself on staying in decent shape, but putting in an honest week of physical labor was tougher than I expected. Still, it was worth it. You should taste the produce here. Asparagus, broccoli, potatoes. And strawberries—oh, man, the strawberries!" Caleb rambled. "I can't figure out what makes everything tastier than anything I've ever grown, if it's the soil or fertilizer…"

"You sound more like a farmer than a detective," Ryan replied, cutting to the chase. "Have you turned up anything interesting in regard to the coins?"

Caleb hesitated. "No, but I've eliminated the cabins as potential hiding places, so that's a start. I think if the thief stowed anything on the property, it must be in the woods. Don't worry, I'll keep looking. How's Liam?"

"Great. Today he swam the length of the community pool without stopping," Ryan said. "That's one good thing about my suspension—I get to spend a lot more time with him. Surprisingly, Sheryl has agreed I can have him on Wednesdays, as well as on the weekends."

That was because she got together with her friends for scrapbooking on Wednesdays, Caleb thought, but he didn't say it. Ryan had a tendency to interpret any small concession on Sheryl's part as a signal she wanted to reconcile, and Caleb didn't want to burst his bubble. Ryan needed to stay optimistic. "I wish I could take Liam swimming in Serenity Lake. It's gorg—" Caleb was interrupted by a sharp rapping. "Uh-oh, gotta go," he whispered and slipped the phone under his pillow before opening the door. Rose was standing on the step, holding a stack of linens. Sweat trickled down both sides of Caleb's neck.

"Is everything okay?" she inquired.

Borrowing a line from her, he replied, "*Jah*, why do you ask?"

"It's awfully hot to have your cabin all sealed up. I thought maybe it meant you had the chills."

"*Neh*, I'm fine," he stated without further explanation. "Are those linens for me?"

"*Jah*, I forgot to ask Charity and Hope to remove your dirty sheets and make up your bed for you today when they changed the guests' bedding. *Muundaag* is laundry day so I can strip the bed for you now if you want—"

"*Neh!* I'll do it myself," Caleb exclaimed, thinking of his cell phone tucked beneath his pillow. "I'd prefer you *meed* not *kumme* inside my cabin."

Rose was taken aback by Caleb's vehement response. Did he think it was inappropriate for her to be alone with him in the cabin? That was why she was going to suggest he could take a walk—but he hadn't let her finish talking. She sure hoped he didn't think she was behaving coquettishly, the way Eleanor had been acting. "Okay, I'll leave these with you and you can bring your dirty linens and clothes to the *haus* by *Muundaag* morning."

"Denki," he said as Rose scurried away.

There had been no mistaking the look of relief on his face when Rose had said she was leaving. She was abashed to remember that, after changing the sheets, she'd planned to invite him to join her on the porch of the main house for tea and dessert. Hope and Charity had gone out bowling, so this was the first real break Rose had taken all week. She was drained, but at least her jam-making efforts were paying off; of the forty-eight jars of jam she'd made that week, she had sold all but seventeen.

A guest had bought a dozen jars to take home to her family and friends as souvenirs of her trip. However, the woman expressed disappointment there wasn't a label on the jar indicating who'd made it. She told Rose, "I think if people knew the jam was homemade by an Amish woman, they'd realize I was giving them something special. Of course, once they taste it they'll realize how special it is anyway, but, you know..."

Rose did know. The woman was suggesting she could sell even more jam if she changed the packaging. And since increasing her sales was exactly what Rose wanted to do, she spent the rest of the evening sketching a design for the labels. She was so excited about her final logo that by Sunday morning she'd forgotten all about her awkward interaction with Caleb.

She and the twins met him outside the barn, where he'd already hitched the horse and buggy and was standing beside the carriage waiting for them to go to church together. A rivulet of perspiration ran from his temples along his hairline even though the day had dawned cool and dry. He asked if Rose wanted to take the reins.

"Jah," she answered. The girls climbed into the back

of the buggy, and she and Caleb sat up front. "Are you sure you're not feverish? You look a little peaked."

"I—I guess I'm a little nervous about attending worship services," he admitted as he donned his hat, which Rose noticed was the same straw hat he'd worn all week. "I'm not sure you'll do things at *kurrich* the same way we do them in Wisconsin and I don't want to offend anyone."

She assured him, "There's only one big difference here in Maine—we meet in a building instead of in each other's homes. But otherwise, I think you'll find *kurrich* here is very similar to Old Order services in Wisconsin. The *leit* are very *freindlich* but you're *wilkom* to sit with us so you won't feel awkward about not knowing anyone yet."

Ordinarily, the twins sat with a group of their female friends, while Nancy, Sol and Rose sat together as a family, but Rose had already privately requested Charity and Hope sit with her and Caleb today. Since she wasn't related to him, she would have felt uncomfortable sitting with him alone, something not even courting couples did. As it turned out, though, the deacon's sermon on God's sovereignty was so thought provoking it wouldn't have mattered where Rose was seated; she was entirely absorbed in what he was saying and she completely lost track of her surroundings.

The worship services were followed by a light lunch during which time the men ate with men and, after serving the men and children, the women ate with women. As she brought a pitcher of water to the men's table, Rose noticed they were including Caleb in their lively conversation and when she caught his eye, he nodded at her as if to confirm she'd been right about how friendly everyone was. Maybe now he'd relax a little, she hoped, realizing she'd be nervous, too, if she went to Wisconsin or someplace where she didn't have any friends or family.

After they'd eaten, Charity and Hope hurried off to spend the afternoon playing volleyball with their friends. Caleb and Rose decided they'd leave, too, and they were heading toward Sol and Nancy's buggy when Eleanor traipsed across the lawn with her brother at her side.

"Caleb! Rose!" she beckoned. After introducing Caleb to Henry, she raved, "Isn't it pleasant out? Not too humid, not too breezy. My *bruder* and I were just saying we think it's a great day to go canoeing."

"Jah," Caleb agreed. "It sure is."

"Terrific!" Eleanor exclaimed. "Henry and I will go home and change, then we'll meet you and Rose down by the dock."

Inwardly Rose groaned. If Eleanor and Caleb wanted to spend time together that was fine with her, but Rose had no intention of being stuck with Henry all afternoon. "I'm kind of tired so I just planned to laze around on the porch and soak in the sunshine. You three will have to navigate the lake without me."

"I'm kind of tired, too," Henry said. "I'll hang out with you instead, Rose."

This situation had just gone from bad to worse and it was all Caleb's fault!

Later, when she was alone with him in the buggy, she accusingly asked why he'd do such a thing.

"Do what?"

"Invite Eleanor and Henry canoeing? If you wanted to go off alone with Eleanor, be my guest, but don't expect me to entertain Henry all afternoon."

"Wait a second! For one thing, I didn't *invite* them canoeing. I only agreed it was a pleasant day. For another thing, I'd like to explore the lake, *jah*, but not because I want to *go off alone* with Eleanor," he said. "And as far as Henry goes, if you don't want him around, why don't you just tell him that outright? You don't seem to have any problem letting me know when you don't want *me* around."

Rose's mouth dropped open. She was aware she'd had a few uncharitable *thoughts* about Caleb, but had she actually come across as that intolerant of his presence? Ashamed, she admitted, "You're right. It's not your fault they're coming over. Eleanor would have contrived a way to *kumme* even if it was raining cats and dogs. And I haven't meant to make you feel unwelcome. I think I've been so caught up in… Well, it doesn't matter, there's no excuse. I'm very sorry."

Even Caleb's profile was handsome, especially when he smiled. "It's okay. I think I have a solution that will help us both out of this predicament."

"I'm all ears."

"You and I will go together in one canoe and they can go in the other. I'll do all the paddling, so you can sit back and relax."

Rose giggled. She liked the way Caleb thought, but he was underestimating how persistent Eleanor and Henry could be. "Those two will never agree to this."

"They won't have a choice if we get to the lake and claim our canoe first."

Grinning, Rose flicked the horse's reins. "Giddyap," she urged.

Chapter Three

"What are you doing out there, Rose? I thought you were tired!" Eleanor wailed. Rose and Caleb waved to her and Henry from where they were idly rocking in the water, some thirty-five feet from shore.

"Why do you think I'm letting Caleb paddle by himself?" Rose answered back.

Caleb smiled. He got the sense Rose didn't relinquish the oars, the reins, the kitchen or any other kind of control very easily. She must *really* not have wanted to spend time alone with Henry if she was willing to let Caleb take charge.

Henry unlaced his boots swiftly and took off his socks as Eleanor sullenly dragged her feet across the sand, her arms crossed against her chest. When she finally climbed into the bow of the canoe and Henry pushed them off from shore, she scolded, "Careful! You're going to tip us over!"

"Which way first?" Caleb asked as the brother and sister neared him and Rose.

Henry pointed to the right. "We'll work our way around the lake counterclockwise."

As Caleb paddled, Rose explained that her aunt and uncle had bought their camp from a wealthy, eccentric *Englischer* who owned all of the land surrounding the one-hundred-and-fifty-acre lake. Mrs. Hallowell also owned a summer mansion on the opposite side of the water, but in the past, whenever her children and grandchildren had come to visit, they'd preferred to rough it together as a large group at "the camp," which Mrs. Hallowell's parents had built for her and her siblings when they were youngsters. Eventually, the brood stopped vacationing there when her children's offspring began attending college. Although Mrs. Hallowell had received countless offers on the property, she'd refused to sell it because she feared developers would turn the land into one giant parking lot and ruin the "rustic charm" of the little structures by building a resort.

According to Rose, Sol had first met the owner when he'd answered an advertisement looking for a farmer and groundskeeper the final summer Mrs. Hallowell's family got together there. They'd struck up such a good rapport that a year or two later she sold the camp to him and Nancy, knowing the Amish wouldn't even install electricity in the cabins, much less build up the property or allow motorboats on the lake. Granted, Mrs. Hallowell still owned virtually all of the property surrounding the lake, but Nancy and Sol had acquired the camp and the acreage near the main road.

Observing the tall pines and rocky inclines bordering the water, Caleb grew overwhelmed—how would he ever search it all? "Does Mrs. Hallowell allow you and your guests to go ashore on her property?"

"*Jah*, but only in designated areas." Rose explained they were welcome to disembark at either of the lake's two small islands, a clearing near a rock the Amish referred to as Relaxation Rock, and at a smaller area leading to a trail up a ridge called Paradise Point.

"What would happen if someone went ashore where they weren't supposed to?" Caleb asked.

"No one is going to shoot you, if that's what you're worried about," Rose said with a laugh. "But when Mrs. Hallowell comes to stay, she does allow her dogs to roam freely near her home and supposedly they're pretty fierce. Plus, she installed surveillance cameras in the woods and at her mansion. It's a common practice among the *Englisch* here. If owners aren't year-round residents they feel they need to make sure no one is breaking into their homes or vandalizing the area while they're away. Mrs. Hallowell told my *ant* and *onkel* about the cameras because she knows how the Amish feel about photography. But it's not an issue because we don't trespass on her land, and out of respect for our beliefs, she disabled the cameras in the places we're allowed to disembark."

Surveillance cameras? Surely the FBI would have obtained the footage from Mrs. Hallowell, right? Since they hadn't found any evidence, Caleb figured he could likely rule out searching the grounds near her mansion and focus on scoping out the areas where there were no cameras. "But how do your guests know where they're allowed to go and where they aren't?"

"There are no-trespassing signs. And information about where they *can* go is included in the guests' *wilkom* pamphlet."

"*Wilkom* pamphlet?" Caleb repeated. That might provide other helpful information…

"*Jah.* We didn't give you one because you're not a

guest, but don't worry. We'll show you where you can go without getting in trouble," Rose teased him over her shoulder.

"There it is, Relaxation Rock," Eleanor announced from behind them. "Let's stop and get out."

Once they pulled their canoes ashore, the foursome went around to the opposite side of the boulder, where its numerous cracks and rounded shape allowed them to scale it easily, even without footwear. The rock had a flat top, which Henry claimed made it an ideal location for picnicking or napping, although more adventurous Amish teenagers—those who could swim—preferred to use the level surface as a platform for plunging into the water ten feet below.

"That path you see over there leads to a dirt road and the dirt road takes you to the main highway," he explained, pointing to an opening through the woods. "Cars are prohibited on the dirt road, but Mrs. Hallowell lets us hitch our buggies at the other end of the path. The district keeps a cart there so the *leit* can wheel in rowboats and canoes when they *kumme* fishing."

Eleanor added, "The last Saturday in August before Labor Day weekend, the camp hosts a fish fry and canoe race for our settlement. Sometimes people *kumme* from Unity, too. Relaxation Rock is where the race begins."

"Sounds like *schpass*. I wonder if I'll be around for it," Caleb commented before he realized what he was saying.

"Why wouldn't you be? Didn't Nancy and Sol tell you the camp is still open then?" Eleanor asked but she didn't wait for an answer. "See, once the guests depart on that Saturday—I think it's August 27 this year—the next guests aren't allowed in until the following Monday so we have the camp completely to ourselves. Everyone has a *wunderbaar* time."

"*Gut.* I'll look forward to it," Caleb said.

Henry smacked an insect against his arm. "The blackflies are eating me alive. Let's go." He scooted to the edge of the rock and slid down the way they'd come up. Eleanor and Caleb followed, and Rose was last. As Henry pushed his canoe into the shallows, Eleanor scampered over to Caleb's canoe and planted herself on the seat in the front.

"C'mon, Caleb," she wheedled sweetly, handing him the paddle. "I want to show you where Kissing Cove is."

Rose had no choice but to join Henry in his canoe. She was glad he didn't paddle as quickly as Caleb because from this distance she couldn't hear Eleanor flirting. For some reason, it really grated on her nerves. Realizing she legitimately *was* a bit weary, Rose exhaled heavily and rode in silence with her eyelids lowered until they arrived at so-called Kissing Cove, fittingly named by the Amish youth who found the secluded area perfect for a little romantic privacy.

"It's too rocky to paddle any closer to shore," Henry warned. "How about if we race to Paradise Point?"

Always up for a challenge, Rose taunted, "*Jah*, last team there is pair of pungent pickerel!"

Henry and Rose hadn't journeyed as far into the cove as Caleb and Eleanor, and they had a head start on their way out. Henry must have been saving his strength because suddenly they glided through the water, agile as a loon. Caleb, however, was even more vigorous, and within a few minutes he and Eleanor pulled alongside them. Rose scooped handfuls of water sideways, causing Eleanor to squeal. Caleb used his paddle to splash back at Rose, and in the process he somehow managed to knock off his own hat and had to reverse in order to pluck it from where it floated on the water's surface.

"What took you so long?" Rose jeered impishly when the couple eventually joined her and Henry onshore near the trail marker for Paradise Point. "You're all wet. Did you fall in?"

"Voll schpass," Caleb replied, flashing those shiny white teeth at her.

She fetched a bag of paper cups and a thermal jug from his canoe. Rose and Eleanor perched on a fallen log, and Caleb and Henry leaned against individual rocks as they drank the sun-brewed mint iced tea Rose had brought. When they were done, she collected the used cups to discard at the camp and picked up a crushed beer can nearby, too.

"One of the guests must have left this, even though we warn them not to litter," she explained to Caleb. "We don't want our hiking privileges revoked."

"Anyone want to jog up to the Point?" Henry asked, obviously showing off.

His sister objected. "Barefoot? No way. My feet are too tender and Caleb already has blisters. We'll stay here, but you and Rose can go ahead if you'd like to."

"I *wouldn't* like to," Rose said. She was sick of Eleanor trying to fob off her brother so she could be alone with Caleb. "I'm getting *hungerich* and I want to go back to the *haus*. It's our turn to race. You against me, Eleanor."

"No fair," the younger woman whined. "You're a lot

more muscular than I am. Look how broad your shoulders are compared to mine!"

Oh, brother. If Eleanor was trying to be insulting, she'd have to try harder than that. Rose liked her athletic build, and she carried herself with confidence. Turning Eleanor's words around, she admitted, "You're right, you probably *are* a lot weaker than I am. I'll just have to race Caleb instead."

Caleb looked amused. "You think you're up for that?"

"I could beat you blindfolded."

"You're on," Caleb agreed. "Eleanor, hand me your kerchief, please."

"Why?"

"Rose thinks she can beat me blindfolded."

"That was a figure of speech," Rose said. "I'm not really going to race you blindfolded."

"Afraid you'll lose?" Caleb's eyes twinkled charmingly, but not irresistibly.

"I'm not *afraid* of anything," Rose declared. "But if one of the canoes capsizes and sinks, I'll have to replace it."

"C'mon, Rose, this will be *schpass*," Henry spurred her on. "Nothing will happen to the canoes. I'll direct you straight to shore. Trust me."

"Rose doesn't trust *anyone*," Eleanor goaded.

Bristling, Rose responded by taking a seat in the bow of the canoe and placing the paddle across her knees. Then she unpinned her kerchief and folded it into a long rectangle to tie over her eyes. Caleb sat down and began to do the same with Eleanor's head covering.

"No peeking," he warned.

Rose stuck her tongue out at him before she realized he couldn't see her anyway.

"On your mark, get set, go!" Eleanor yelled, and Rose paddled with all her might.

"Go, Rose, go!" Henry yelled. "Right, paddle on your right side! Now left. Left."

Rose followed his instructions but she could barely hear him over Eleanor's screams. "Hurry, Caleb, hurry! You're passing her, you're passing her!"

Fighting the urge to laugh—this really was a crazy thing to be doing, and it was a lot of fun—Rose pulled through the water in deep, hard strokes, her muscles burning until Henry finally announced, "We're almost there. This is the final stretch, Rose! We're winning—"

Not five seconds later, Caleb and Eleanor's canoe knocked into theirs so forcefully Rose felt like her molars were vibrating. She lurched sideways, nearly toppling into the water. When she peeled the kerchief from her eyes she saw they were headed straight for a rock that peaked just below the water's surface. There was no time to change course and she winced as it scraped against the hull of the canoe, nearly bringing them to a standstill as they passed over it.

Onshore, Eleanor was getting out of the canoe, shouting, "You did it, Caleb! We won!"

Caleb paid her no attention. "Are you okay?" he called to Henry and Rose.

"We're fine, but I'm not so sure about the boat," Henry replied.

Rose propelled them the rest of the way to shore, where Caleb and Henry flipped the canoe to take a look. Sure enough, a gouge marred the hull and a deep scratch ran half the length of the vessel. *And* this *is ex-*

actly what happens when you blindly trust someone, Rose thought. "Great, just what I needed—one more thing to try to rebuild," she uttered in disgust.

Too exasperated to say anything else, she stormed toward the house, but not before Eleanor remarked to Caleb, "Kind of a sore loser, isn't she?"

Caleb pressed his fingertips gently against the dent on the canoe's hull, but it didn't give way—a good sign. It meant the damage was mostly cosmetic and he could easily fix it if he picked up a few supplies. He asked Henry to help him carry the canoe to the barn since he didn't want any of the guests using it until it was repaired.

"I hope Rose doesn't blame me for causing her to run over the rock. It's not my fault we bumped into them," Eleanor insisted as she trailed after the men. "I couldn't see around you, Caleb, so I didn't know we were about to collide."

"If it's anyone's fault, it's mine," Caleb reassured her. "I shouldn't have suggested we race like that in the first place. But, uh, right now Rose seems pretty upset and it's time for me to *millich* the *kuh*, so—"

Henry got the message. "*Jah*, we should leave now. We'll go get our shoes and, uh, can you tell Rose I said *mach's gut*?"

"Sure," Caleb agreed. *If she's still talking to me.*

"See you tomorrow, Caleb," Eleanor said. "I hope Rose doesn't chew you out too bad."

I hope the same thing. When he had finished with the evening milking, Caleb brought the pail to the house, but Rose didn't answer the door. Since he didn't want to spoil more milk by leaving it outside in the heat again, he opened the door and called, "Rose?"

She must have been upstairs or in the bathroom because she didn't answer, so Caleb tentatively scanned the entryway. A few feet farther inside was a narrow desk, and atop of it a notebook labeled Reservations caught his eye. *Aha!* He tiptoed to the desk. With trembling hands, he flipped the book open to scan the entries. He wasn't sure how he would identify the strangely behaved couple's names or cabin number, but he figured any information he could glean would be helpful.

"What are you doing?" Rose demanded, leaning over the banister halfway down the stairs. He slapped the book closed without finding the late-May entries.

"I, uh, brought in the *millich*. You didn't *kumme* to the door when I knocked or called so I let myself in."

"I can see that. But why are you rifling through that paperwork?"

"I wanted… I wanted one of the *wilkom* pamphlets you told me about." It wasn't an outright lie—Caleb *did* want a welcome pamphlet—but this time he somehow felt guiltier for misleading her than when he'd given vague responses to Rose's other questions.

She bustled down the stairs, reached in front of him and pulled a tri-fold sheet of paper from a folder beneath the reservation book. "Here."

"Denki." He exchanged the pail for the paper. "I also wanted to say I'm really sorry about the canoe. I'll pay for the supplies to repair it—which I'll do myself. The damage is minimal. I'll have it shipshape again by midday tomorrow."

She peered at him through narrowed eyes. "I'd appreciate that and so will our guests." She moved toward the door and held it open, obviously dismissing him.

Ordinarily he would have beaten a path back to his cabin, but Caleb felt compelled to get back on better terms with Rose again. "So, uh, does this mean you're not making me any supper?"

Shifting the milk pail to her other hand, she kept the door propped open with her foot. "Seriously?" She arched an eyebrow at him. "You've got some nerve, you know that?"

He shrugged. "What can I say? I'm *hungerich* and your meals are the highlight of my day."

Watching the smile come over Rose's face was like watching a flower open. "Fine," she conceded. "Since it's the *Sabbat*, we're just having leftovers. You can wait on the porch while I prepare them."

Caleb hummed as he rocked in the glider and reveled in the view of the lake until Rose emerged from the house with a tray. He immediately recognized the dish as being Amish haystack, which was a combination of cooked hamburger and pork mixed with tomato sauce and chopped vegetables—asparagus and broccoli in this case—served on a bed of lettuce and topped with melted cheese. Somehow, no matter what was included in the mishmash of ingredients, a haystack dinner always turned out to be delectable, and Caleb was glad Rose hadn't skimped on their portions. He was even gladder to see the tray also contained two slices of strawberry-rhubarb pie.

"So Hope and Charity still aren't home?" he asked, his mouth half-full.

"*Neh*, not yet. I hope they don't stay out too late. Their *rumspringa* began a couple months ago. They're bright, sensible, Godly *meed*, but they're also a little naive about people's intentions. I don't want them to wind up hurt because someone has taken advantage of them."

Caleb forced himself to stop eating long enough to comment, "I understand your concern. If I had *gschwischderkinner* like Charity and Hope, I'd want to shield them from the influence of *Englisch* teenagers, too."

"*Englisch* teenagers? It's not the *Englischers* who worry me—it's their Amish peers. Just because they're Amish doesn't mean their behavior is always honorable, you know." Rose's expression clouded. "And that goes for me, too… I'm sorry I was so short-tempered about the canoe cracking. I know it was an accident."

"*Jah*, but I shouldn't have badgered you into racing blindfolded. You didn't want to."

"Only because if anything goes wrong at the camp, it's ultimately my responsibility to fix it." Rose chewed her bottom lip as she served him a slice of pie. "As a business owner, I haven't always made wise decisions, so I'm trying to change that."

"You own a business?"

"I used to. A restaurant. But, well, I had to give up my lease." She picked a crumb from where it had fallen on her lap, her voice brightening as she added, "I intend to rent a new place in the fall if I can afford it. That's why I've been making so much jam—I'm trying to earn more money on the side to cover what I'll need for a down payment on the café."

Aha. So that explained why Rose sometimes seemed so uptight; she was financially pressured. Caleb felt honored she had confided in him. Smacking his lips, he laid down his fork. "If it's money you need, you really ought to consider selling pies, not jam. People can polish off a pie quicker than they can consume a jar of jam. With dessert this tasty, they'd be coming back for more the next day. You'd make a fortune."

Rose would have been inclined to think Caleb was flattering her again, but he'd devoured his pie with such gusto she believed he genuinely meant what he said. "That's actually not a bad suggestion."

"*Jah*, it sure beats my idea about canoeing blindfolded," he joked, making her giggle. Then his forehead wrinkled with sincerity as he apologized again, "I really am sorry about that. Like I said, I can fix the damage right away, but that means I'll need to take the buggy into town tomorrow morning."

If Rose was going to make pies, she'd need to buy ingredients and aluminum foil pie plates, and she also had to make a deposit at the bank, so she said she'd like to accompany Caleb. They were working out a mutually agreeable time to go when Charity and Hope came around the side of the house—one of their friends must have dropped them off near the barn—and plodded up the stairs. They looked upset.

Caleb seemed to notice their frowns, too. "Hello, you two," he said. "Is something wrong?"

They exchanged glances before Charity responded. "First of all, we really were playing volleyball at Miriam Lapp's *haus* for most of the afternoon..." she began.

Rose was instantly alarmed. "But?"

"But afterward we went to Black Bear Lake. Miriam knows some *Englisch* kids whose *eldre* let them use their speedboats. So we cruised around for a while with them."

Although it gave her the chills to imagine her young cousins tooling around a crowded lake in a speedboat with a teenager at the helm, Rose resisted the urge to express her disapproval. She didn't want to make Charity and Hope reluctant to talk openly with her in the future. Besides, the girls were such hard workers, and with their father being so ill for so long, Rose was glad they'd been enjoying a little summer recreation with their friends. "Was someone hurt?" she asked as calmly as she could manage.

"*Neh*, nothing like that happened. We were really careful—we all wore life vests," Hope assured her, fidgeting. "But one of the *Englisch* kids, Oliver Graham, made a point of telling the other *Englischers* we were the ones whose camp was raided by the FBI."

"Jah," Charity chimed in. "Oliver said the thieves they were looking for are drug abusers who stayed at our camp and that they're still hanging out in the area. He claimed *Mamm* and *Daed* covered for them because they're afraid of what'll happen to us if they turn them in."

Rose went off on an uncensored tirade. "That's absolute *hogwash*! First of all, your *mamm* and *daed* told the authorities everything they knew. Secondly, nothing ever came of the FBI's search—and if you or anyone else was ever in danger, they definitely would have warned us. Furthermore, didn't you hear what the deacon said in church today about how nothing happens outside of *Gott*'s sovereign will? That *baremlich bu* was just being a pest. I can't understand why he'd want to scare you like that, but what he said is complete rubbish."

"See?" Charity said to Hope. For Rose and Caleb's benefit, she explained, "I told Hope Oliver was being vengeful because when he asked her to go in his speedboat alone with him, she turned him down in front of everyone."

"I wasn't trying to embarrass him. I just didn't want to go," Hope said, twisting her mouth to the side.

"You used sound judgment, and there's no need to justify your refusal to go anywhere with any *bu*." Caleb spoke up before Rose could express what would have amounted to the same sentiment. "What did you say his name is?"

Hope hesitated, glancing at Charity again before answering. "Oliver Graham. His *eldre* own Graham Cabins on Black Bear Lake."

"Did he mention how he heard that the thieves were still hanging out in the area?"

Charity shook her head and Hope shrugged, but Rose got the feeling they knew the answer. What was Caleb planning to do? Tell the *bu*'s *eldre* on him? For the twins' sake, she wanted him to drop the subject.

"Why does it matter?" she questioned. "You know how rumors start, especially among kids. The less attention we give that kind of gossip, the better off we'll be. Hope and Charity, I saved you some *boi*. Let's go inside and I'll get it for you."

She thought she'd made her point, but before she could say good-night and follow the girls through the door, Caleb stopped her. "Uh, can I talk to you privately for a minute, Rose?"

"*Jah*, what is it?" Rose raised an eyebrow at Caleb after the girls were out of earshot. He feared he was about to damage his newly established rapport with her, but his concern was too important to leave unspoken.

"You're probably right. What Oliver told the girls was likely a *lecherich* rumor, but I still think we should be on the lookout for anyone whose behavior seems odd."

Rose's mouth dropped open and her eyebrows jumped up in mock horror. "You mean like...like people canoeing blindfolded on the lake?" she whispered furtively.

Caleb wasn't amused. "*Neh*, I mean like strangers on the property."

"The only people who ever come to the camp are our guests or our friends, so I don't think we have anything to worry about."

"Still, I've noticed you don't lock the door to the *haus*..."

"Of course I don't—I go in and out of it all day."

"Exactly! Anyone could wander in while you're gardening or down at the dining hall."

Rose snapped her fingers as if she suddenly remembered something. "*Jah*, you're right. Just this evening a man drifted into the *haus*. He claimed to be bringing me *millich* and looking for a *wilkom* pamphlet, but he had a funny accent. Clearly he wasn't from around here. Maybe I should call the police?"

Any other time, Caleb would have responded with a wisecrack of his own, but tonight he frowned. "Rose, I'm serious."

Her levity extinguished, Rose huffed. "As I said, my *ant* and *onkel* told the agents and detectives everything they knew, and law enforcement was satisfied there was never any thief staying here. As for someone wandering into the *haus*, the only cash on-site is what we receive from guests when they check in on *Samschdaag*. And I keep that money well hidden until I can deposit it at the bank, usually the following *Muundaag.* I doubt the earnings from our produce stand and my jam would be enough to entice anyone to steal."

"It's not the money I'm concerned about. It's you and the *meed*—"

"Whatever happened to you telling my *onkel* Sol you thought I could chase away any unsavory characters myself?"

"I meant guys from *kurrich*, not potential thieves or drug abusers. You can't be too careful, you know."

"You sound like an *Englischer.* What's next? Is locking our doors being prudent enough or should we install surveillance cameras the way Mrs. Hallowell does?" she gibed. "As I said, we *do* take precautions, but beyond that, we have to believe the Lord will watch over us."

"I *do* believe that. But I also believe the Lord wants us to be *gut* stewards of our resources. To safeguard what He's given us—including our lives."

Rose exhaled loudly. "Listen, I'm not going to lock the door during the day—with everything else I have to do, I can't be bothered to keep track of a key, too. I don't even know if Nancy *has* a key. But I will start locking up at night while we're sleeping, and I'll ask the *meed* to do the same."

They hadn't been locking their house at night while they were inside asleep? Caleb shivered. "*Denki.* That will help put my mind at ease."

But the conversation actually heightened his anxiety. As soon as he got back to his cabin, he closed the windows and door and called Ryan to report what Hope and Charity had told him. "If the thief really is hanging around nearby and he decides to come back here, I'm concerned things could get dangerous."

"I wouldn't give a teenager's gossip much credence. Remember the kinds of stories that used to circulate when we were kids?" Ryan countered. "Think about it—why would the thief send me a note indicating the coins are at the camp if he was going to come back and collect them himself?"

Caleb rubbed the sweat from his forehead and looked at his hand absentmindedly before rubbing it on his trousers. "Maybe it wasn't the thief who wrote the note. It could have been an accomplice who got cold feet or who turned on his partner."

There was a weighted silence before Ryan replied. "I still think it's just gossip, but I wouldn't want to put you in harm's way. If you're uncomfortable, you should leave."

Caleb could hear the heaviness in Ryan's voice; he didn't want to let him down. And now Caleb had another concern to consider: If he left, who would keep an eye out for Rose and the twins? Even if Rose thought they *were* in danger, she probably wouldn't go to the police, so there was no chance she'd go now, when she scoffed at the suggestion she needed to be careful. At least if Caleb stayed here, he could monitor the situation. "I can't leave yet. It's too soon," he told his brother. *And I'm already in too deep.*

Chapter Four

Because Monday was wash day and Rose used her spare time in between making breakfast and lunch to go to town with Caleb, she wasn't able to go berry picking until the afternoon. Kneeling between the long rows of strawberry plants, she had a clear view of the main road, and she was pleased to see how frequently cars either stopped to make purchases or at least slowed down to survey the shelves of fruits and vegetables in the little three-sided shed. It occurred to her that the roadside sign simply said Produce, so she'd need to make another one for drivers to know she was selling pies, as well as fruits and vegetables.

She was thinking about how she wanted the sign to read when someone honked a horn. Glancing up, Rose noticed a tall, slender woman had pulled over by the produce stand. She was leaning into her car's open window and pressing the horn with one hand while waving at Rose with another. When Rose waved back, the woman gestured for her to come to the car. *Ach.* What did she want? The produce stand operated on an honor system, with customers putting their money in the plastic mayonnaise jar used as a till and taking out what was due back to them. Rose hoped the woman wasn't going to ask her to make change for a big bill, because she didn't want to take the time away from picking berries to run back to the house. Rose would rather the woman take the produce now and come back with the money another day.

But the woman apparently wasn't interested in buying anything. "I'm looking for Serenity Lake Cabins," she said. The woman wore bright lipstick and brilliant diamond earrings. Rose never understood the appeal of either; she imagined lipstick felt greasy, like after you'd eaten fried chicken, and that the earrings pinched one's earlobes. Then she caught sight of herself in the woman's dark sunglasses and thought, *I suppose* you *might wonder how* I *can stand to have dirt beneath my fingernails.* She straightened her kerchief.

"The cabins are down there," she said, pointing to the dirt driveway. "I'm managing the camp. What can I do for you?"

The woman grinned; except for a smear of fuchsia across her front tooth, her smile was as white as Caleb's. "I'm Julia, the one who called on Saturday to inquire about a vacancy."

Rose remembered. "Right, but as I told you, we're full for the season."

"I know," the woman replied. "But I hope to stay here next year and I was passing through on my way back to Portland. So I thought I could take a peek at the accommodations."

"I'm sorry, but the cabins are occupied and we can't disturb our guests," Rose said. *Besides, I don't have the time to show you around.*

Julia pouted. "Really? I couldn't find any information about the camp on the internet, and I don't really want to rent sight unseen."

"I understand, but—"

"I won't disturb anyone, I promise. It's just that this is the only time I'll be in the area this summer so I made a point of stopping by. And I'm glad I did because I want to buy some of this amazing-looking produce before I leave..."

Rose understood what Julia was implying: if Rose let her have her way, the woman would make a purchase. "I suppose I could show you around the grounds," she compromised. "I can't let you inside any of the cabins, but I can give you a pamphlet describing them."

"Denki," the woman said, her pronunciation making it sound like *donkey*, and Rose had to suppress a snicker. "Is it close enough to walk or should we go in my car?"

It would have been quicker to get into the woman's car to drive the quarter of a mile to the camp, but as Rose glanced down at her skirt, she realized it was stained with dirt and strawberry juice, and she probably smelled from perspiring in the afternoon sun. Furthermore, while it was permissible for the Amish to accept a ride from *Englischers*, Rose felt self-conscious about riding in the car such a short distance—it seemed lazy. What would the guests think if they saw her?

"It's just down the driveway. We can walk," Rose said, so the woman grabbed a hat with a big floppy brim from the passenger seat, rolled up the window and pressed her keys to lock the car doors. Unfortunately, Rose noticed too late she was wearing sandals with very high heels and she could take only slow, mincing steps down the uneven dirt lane.

Julia was going to have to purchase a lot of produce to make up for the time Rose was wasting. Immediately, she felt a stitch of remorse at the thought. Her aunt and uncle expected her to be courteous to all guests, and Rose imagined that included future guests, too. She slowed her gait so Julia could keep up.

When they finally made it to the main house, Rose dashed inside and returned with a pamphlet, which she extended to the woman, who had taken a seat in the glider.

"How many cabins are there?" she asked. "I've counted nine."

"Eight—it's all in the pamphlet. We don't rent out that little one. It's the one our groundskeeper stays in." She pointed toward Caleb's cabin.

"Are boats allowed on the lake?"

"We have canoes and rowboats for guests to use, or they can bring their own kayaks. Motorboats are prohibited anywhere on the lake."

"I'd love to see the waterfront," the woman hinted.

Why? You can see the lake as plain as day from here, Rose thought, her patience wearing thin. The "waterfront" was just a little patch of sand. Just then she noticed Caleb rounding the corner and she was suddenly inspired. "I'll ask Caleb to give you a quick tour," she said, waving him over to join them.

Caleb hopped up the porch steps. "Hello," he said. "*Gut* news," he told Rose. "I fixed the canoe and it's dry enough to put in the water." He expected her to be pleased; instead, she winced.

"Caleb, this is Julia," she said. From the angle he'd approached, he hadn't noticed the woman sitting on the other side of where Rose was standing. "She's considering renting a cabin next year."

Caleb immediately understood why Rose had pulled a face. He shouldn't have mentioned the canoe was damaged in front of a potential customer. With a nod to Julia, he said, "If you do, you'll enjoy your stay. It's very peaceful here. And Rose's cooking is delicious." *Although, I can't imagine someone who dresses like you do would like the "rustic charm" of this place. Doesn't look like you eat much, either.*

"Rose said you'd give me a tour of the waterfront," the woman replied.

Rose interjected apologetically, "I know you're busy, but I left a flat of strawberries unattended in the field. I'm afraid the chipmunks will go after them."

A tour of the waterfront? It was no bigger than a child's sandbox and he had a to-do list a mile long. Still, Caleb was flattered Rose entrusted him with the task. Besides, how could he resist her imploring amber eyes? "Sure," he agreed. "I can show Julia the beach. Not that it's very big, but it does provide an unobstructed view of the lake."

Rose's grateful expression was worth the time it took Caleb to accompany Julia down to the lake. Surveying it, Julia peppered him with questions about the hiking trails in the hills encircling the water, how many houses were built on the lake and whether the public had access to it, too. Although he was relieved he'd learned enough about the area to accurately field her questions, Caleb felt conspicuous when Julia remarked, "If you don't mind me saying so, for an Amish person you actually sound like you have a Midwestern accent, you know that?"

"Is that so?" Caleb pivoted to walk toward the main house so Julia couldn't see his face, which he was sure was glowing with embarrassment.

As she painstakingly made her way up the incline, she asked, "So, how long have you and your wife owned this camp?"

"My wife? You mean Rose?" he questioned. "She's not my wife."

The woman stopped in her tracks. "You *live* with her? I didn't think the Amish allow—"

"They *don't*," he said emphatically before she could complete her thought. Then he realized he should have said "*we* don't," since he was supposed to be one of the Amish. Fortunately, the woman was so chatty she didn't seem to notice his error.

"Oh, sorry. I thought this was a family business, so I assumed she was your wife. Is she your sister?"

Caleb felt conflicted about answering. On one hand, he understood in the *Englisch* world her question wouldn't be considered intrusive. On the other hand, he knew the Amish kept their private lives private—especially from *Englischers*. "No, she's not my sister," he said simply. "I have to get back to work now, so we should keep walking."

"Oh! Of course," the woman agreed gamely and continued up the hill. "You go do whatever it is you need to do. I can find my way back to my car myself."

"I need to speak to Rose, so I'm headed that way, too," Caleb said, and, within minutes, he wished he hadn't. He could have completed three or four tasks on his list in the time it took Julia to practically tiptoe down the dirt road. Her shoes were completely inappropriate for the uneven surface and when she stumbled,

Caleb instinctively held out his arm for her to steady herself. She latched on and didn't let go until they arrived at the car.

"Thanks for the tour," she said as she took her hat off and tossed it onto the passenger seat. Flipping her long blond hair over her shoulder, she gave him a once-over and remarked, "I hope I get to see you next summer."

Caleb recognized the sultriness in her tone. He had only been living as an Amish man for a week, and already he was appalled by how brazen the *Englisch* woman seemed to him compared to…to Rose. He eagerly trod across the field to where she was picking strawberries.

"Sorry about mentioning the damaged canoe in front of a potential customer," he said. "But I think she'll end up renting a cabin next year anyway. She seemed to really like it here."

"*Jah*, I noticed. *You* seemed to like her being here, too," Rose retorted without looking up.

Once again, Caleb had thought Rose would be pleased with his efforts, and when she appeared annoyed instead, he began to lose patience. "What, exactly, do you mean by that?"

"I mean you were walking arm in arm with her!" She snapped a rotten strawberry from its stem, briefly inspected it and then chucked it over her shoulder.

She's jealous! The thought gave Caleb a strange twinge of delight.

Then Rose lectured, "I don't know how your district does things in Wisconsin, but here in Serenity Ridge, we don't make a public show of hugging strangers—especially not when they're *Englisch*!"

Caleb's cheeks smarted from the chagrin of realizing

how mistaken he'd been to think Rose was jealous. She didn't envy Julia for holding his arm; she was angry at Caleb for acting in a way that was considered to be disgraceful. Although his first impulse was to argue he hadn't done anything inappropriate, Caleb's anthropology background helped him consider the situation from Rose's perspective. After all, he was supposed to be Amish, and no Amish man he'd ever met would have allowed an *Englisch* woman to clasp his arm like that. It was no wonder Rose was disgusted.

"I wasn't embracing her," he said calmly. "She kept stumbling so I gave her my arm for balance. I thought it was the courteous thing to do for a customer."

"We don't need customers *that* badly," she said, shielding her eyes as she squinted up at him. "What would our guests think if they saw the two of you coming up the driveway like that? It would give them the wrong impression."

"You're right," Caleb admitted. "But I was genuinely afraid she'd twist her ankle or trip and hurt herself. You have no idea how litigious some people can be—"

"Litigious? What does that mean?"

Caleb realized the more he tried to wiggle out of this, the more *Englisch* he seemed. "It refers to someone who likes to bring lawsuits against someone else. I was concerned if she got hurt she might try to sue your *ant* and *onkel*. Try to take away their home and lakeside property. She'd say it was negligence because the road was too bumpy."

"Pah," Rose uttered. She relaxed visibly, sitting back on her heels. "She was the one wearing impractical footwear so she couldn't blame my *ant* and *onkel* for something that wasn't their fault. I doubt anyone would make an unfair accusation like that."

That's because you don't know the Englisch *like I do.* With thoughts of Ryan running through his mind, Caleb replied sorrowfully, "It happens more often than you think."

As Rose looked into Caleb's forlorn eyes in the silence that followed, she regretted having been so angry at him. No, not just angry. When she'd seen him walking with Julia, she felt as if she'd bitten into an unripe strawberry. What was that bitter emotion—jealousy? That was *narrish*. She was not envious of the attention Caleb paid to any woman, especially an *Englischer*. An *Englischer* who, by the way, took up both of their time yet ended up not buying any produce!

While Rose still didn't think it was right of him to allow the woman to wrap her arm through his, she knew she could have brought up the subject in a more tactful way. After all, she appreciated that he had done her a favor by giving Julia the tour, and she told him so. "I shouldn't have asked you to do something that was my responsibility, but I appreciate that you did and you did it so cheerfully. It allowed me to get back to berry picking so I could start on the pies as soon as possible," she said. "The season peaked early this year, and it's just about over now. I need every berry I can get."

"I was *hallich* to help." Caleb crouched down beside her and ran his palms over the tops of the strawberry plants. "Looks like you've almost picked the patch clean."

"Almost, but not quite. I still have to pick all of those rows over there by Wednesday, since it's supposed to rain on Thursday and Friday. The berries always taste washed-out after a hard rain, and if I wait until Saturday they'll be overly ripe," she said.

"I could help you," Caleb offered.

"*Denki*, but it's my endeavor." *And I've learned it's best to manage my business by myself.*

"I don't want any part of the proceeds, if that's what you're worried about."

"That's not it. Still, it wouldn't be fair to accept your help and not share the profit with you. Picking berries for pies I'm going to sell goes above and beyond what's expected of you as an employee."

"What if I just want to help you as a friend?" Caleb plucked a fat berry from its stem, dropped it into the tray and looked back at her. His eyes were *so* blue.

I'm parched, she thought, suddenly woozy. *It must be the sun.* Rose dipped her chin and reached for a berry. "*Denki*, but—"

"But you'd rather not make as much money as you can?" he ribbed her. "If it makes you feel better, you can owe me a favor in return."

"All right, it's a deal," Rose finally conceded. The truth was that she really could use his help, and she was starting to not mind his company, either.

Caleb wasn't sure why he insisted on helping Rose other than being grateful she wasn't holding a grudge against him for his blunder with Julia. Few women he'd ever been in a relationship with had demonstrated that kind of grace before. Not that he was in a relationship with Rose, but he was glad she didn't dismiss his notion they were friends, as well as coworkers.

He started picking at the beginning of the row next

to her, and he worked so fast he quickly caught up to where she was, so that they were kneeling side by side. As they worked, she told him she was going to make a new sign advertising the pies.

"I saw some paint and a stack of plywood in the barn. You could use that," he suggested. "I'll pull it out for you after supper."

"Denki," she said, stopping to lift a berry to her mouth. She bit into it and closed her eyes, the juice dripping from her fingers. "Mmm, that's *gut.* I was really thirsty," she said. "Is it this hot in the summer in Wisconsin?"

"*Jah*, it can be roasting there, especially because of the humidity. We get some big thunderstorms, too." Weather was a safe topic; Caleb hoped Rose wouldn't question him more about his family or his teaching. He quickly redirected their conversation. "Have you been hiking in the woods here, by the camp?"

"These woods?" She pointed to the areas bordering both sides of the fields and Caleb nodded. "*Neh.* They're too buggy and there aren't any real paths to follow."

"How about on the islands on the lake?"

"*Neh*, I've just paddled around them. Why?"

"I was wondering if they're worth exploring." *If they'd make good hiding places for stolen property...*

"They're pretty small, but I've heard they provide a nice shady place for a picnic or shelter from the rain if you're out fishing and can't get back to the camp in time. But Paradise Point is my favorite place to get out. It's a steep climb, but the view makes it worth it. It was too bad we weren't wearing shoes on Sunday or we could have gone to the top."

"Maybe next time," Caleb suggested, figuring it

would be helpful to his search if he went with someone who was already familiar with the landscape. And better Rose than Eleanor. Or Henry. Or anybody else, for that matter.

"Mmm-hmm," Rose murmured distractedly. It wasn't a commitment, but it was better than a refusal.

Whistling, Caleb continued picking berries so swiftly he soon moved far ahead of Rose in the parallel row, which made further conversation impractical.

"Show-off," she called to him some forty minutes later. "It's almost quitting time. I need to make supper pretty soon."

"You go ahead. I'm fine here alone."

"*Neh*, I can't leave until you do. That wouldn't be right."

"Just five more minutes then. There are lots of ripe ones over here," he bargained.

It must have been fifteen minutes later when he felt a little thump between his shoulder blades. Then another one a few inches lower. "Hey!" he shouted. As he stood and turned toward her, Rose lobbed a rotten strawberry right at his chest. Then at his head. Apparently she had stockpiled the unusable fruit in a fold in her apron and was chucking them at him in rapid fire. His white shirt was already grimy, and now it bloomed with crimson.

He bent to retrieve the berries she'd thrown and tossed them back at her. One caught her right in the forehead and another bounced off her arm. They volleyed fruit back and forth until finally she held her palm up and yelled, *"Absatz!"*

"Then drop what you have in your apron," he demanded.

"You drop what you have in your hand first."

"Why? Don't you trust me?" Although Caleb had been teasing, to his surprise Rose let her apron fall flat. The mushy berries spilled to the ground for the birds to enjoy later.

"I'm beginning to," she said, wiping juice from her forehead with the back of her hand. "Truce?"

Caleb opened his fists, letting the fruit bounce at his feet. "Truce," he said, smiling. Contention between him and a woman had never been such fun.

After Caleb scraped the last bit of cheesy sauce from his plate, Rose stood and prompted the girls. "Let's get these dishes cleared. I've got a big tray of strawberries to wash, hull and quarter." She intended to sell pies only on the day she made them, which meant she'd have to wake by four thirty on Tuesday morning. By preparing all of her ingredients this evening, she'd ensure she had enough time to bake the pies before starting breakfast for the camp guests.

"I took the plywood out of the barn and brought it to the house," Caleb said as he pushed the bench back so he could rise. "I brought up a pint of paint and a brush, too."

"*Ach!* I forgot all about my sign. *Denki* for doing that for me. I'll have to get to it in the morning."

"It won't be dry enough to put out on the roadside if you wait until the morning. I'll do it for you," Caleb offered.

Rose touched her hairline. There was something sticky there even though she'd washed her face after her strawberry fight with Caleb. "You just want me to owe you another favor," she teased.

"*Neh*, there's no payback necessary. Although, if you

felt inclined to make a spare pie for the staff to eat, I wouldn't object."

Rose chuckled. "I was going to make one for us anyway."

"*Ach*, then I should have asked for two," Caleb said, snapping his fingers. "What do you want the sign to say? Pies Made by an Amish Rose?"

Even though Rose was her name, there was something about the way Caleb called her *an Amish Rose* that made it difficult for her to meet his eyes. "I guess it should just say Rose's Pies." She added, "*Denki.* I appreciate your help—again."

And she did, at the same time aware she couldn't let it become a habit. It wouldn't be fair to accept Caleb's help without compensating him in some way, especially since she realized he was running off so fast because he had to complete chores their berry picking had prevented him from finishing that afternoon. So, later, when she was measuring the ingredients she'd need for the crusts, she was sure to include enough extra to make a batch of individual-sized pies just for him as a token of appreciation, as well as an extra pie for all the staff to share together.

After she'd prepared the berries and taken the remaining rhubarb she'd frozen out of the freezer, she set out the other ingredients and mixing bowls. She was rummaging through the cupboards in search of extra pie tins when she thought she heard the dining hall screen door creak open. "Hello?" she called, but no one answered. *All that sunshine I got today must be playing tricks with my mind*, she thought and stopped to drink a glass of water.

By the time she left the dining hall, it was almost ten

o'clock. All of the guests' cabins were dark, and from the direction of the lake, a loon cried. The sound was so eerily beautiful it made Rose shiver. She was almost to the house when something rustled loudly in the thicket of bushes on the side of the path. "Is someone there?" she asked. A branch snapped and then there was utter silence, which for some reason was even more unsettling. Was something—or someone—watching her? Rose fled up the porch steps, entered the house, slammed the door behind her and quickly turned the bolt.

"What's wrong?" Charity asked as she descended the stairs.

Rose panted. "Nothing. I'm probably being *lappich*. I heard something in the bushes and my imagination ran away with me." It was Caleb's influence—all that talk about criminals lurking nearby.

"It could have been the moose. Miriam's *daed* saw it on *Freidaag* morning." There was at least one young bull moose known to roam Serenity Ridge, but Rose doubted that was what she'd heard.

"*Neh*, it wasn't loud enough to be a moose—and a moose wouldn't have suddenly stopped walking, either. It was probably one of the guests. Or a raccoon." But now she would check to see if the back door was locked, too.

Fortunately, Rose's fatigue overshadowed her trepidation, and she fell asleep quickly and slept soundly until morning. When she headed toward the dining hall at first light, she noted deer tracks on the path and felt foolish about her jitteriness the evening before. As she rolled out the pie dough, she prayed for her aunt and uncle and asked *Gott* to bless her efforts that day, especially with her pie making. She thanked the Lord for Caleb's help, too. Ah, Caleb. *He's not at all like I thought he was the first time I met him*, she thought. *I guess that's what* Ant *Nancy meant by giving him a chance to demonstrate his character instead of judging him.*

Thanks to the large oven, Rose was able to make half a dozen pies before breakfast. After the guests had been served and she, Caleb and the girls had eaten, Rose retrieved the little wagon from the side of the house to cart the pies, jarred goods and any produce still fresh enough to sell to the roadside stand. Caleb walked with her, carrying her new sign. "The pies will sell out by noon, you'll see," he said.

Later, as she was restocking the shelves with freshly picked vegetables, she discovered he was right—all of the pies were gone and it wasn't even lunchtime yet. The early success motivated her to pick berries again that afternoon and she gladly accepted Caleb's help. Not only did he pick even faster than she did, but talking to him made the work seem less tedious. While she noticed he asked more questions than he answered, she figured since his parents had died, talking about family made him lonely, so she didn't push.

On Wednesday the pies sold out by ten thirty—Rose couldn't keep herself from checking the produce stand every hour or so—and that afternoon Caleb joined her in the strawberry patch again, which was a good thing, since a torrential rain broke out at suppertime. "Looks like we picked all the *gut* berries in the nick of time," she commented, telling Caleb she'd freeze the surplus strawberries or keep them in the cool of the basement so she could make strawberry-raspberry pies the following week, when she hoped the raspberries would be ripe enough to pick.

"I doubt any *boi* could taste as delectable as your *ae-*

beer babrag boi, but I'm willing to be proved wrong," Caleb offered. "Rarely happens, though."

"Nice try," Rose countered, but she'd already decided she'd make a few individual-sized strawberry-raspberry pies for him to sample.

On Friday morning, as she rolled the wagon to the stand, Rose noticed a car idling near the roadway. A middle-aged woman got out and opened a large green umbrella. "Are you Rose?" she asked.

"I am." Rose didn't mind the rain and she'd covered the wagon with a big piece of cardboard so its contents wouldn't get wet, but the woman extended her umbrella to shield Rose's head, too.

"I'm Helen Berton," she said. "We own the Inn on Black Bear Lake."

Rose squinted at her. "How may I help you?"

"I bought a couple of your delicious pies this week and I wanted to put in an order for more. Yesterday someone bought them all before I could get here. Full disclosure—I do serve them to our guests, but meals are included in the cost of their stay, so it's not as if I'm directly reselling or profiting from your pies."

Rose didn't answer right away. She wasn't sure she could commit to taking orders—her first commitment had to be to the guests at the camp. So far nothing had happened to prevent her from making pies to sell, but if there was an issue with a guest or a cabin she had to attend to, Rose might not have time for extra baking. There were always legitimate excuses for an occasional lapse, but it wouldn't reflect well on the Amish—or on Rose—if she agreed to an arrangement and then didn't honor her word. "I don't really take orders. I have more of a first-come, first-served policy," she said.

"Please? I'll pay double what you're charging per pie. They're well worth it."

Now, *that* was tempting. Maybe if Rose shared her concern about something urgent arising at the camp they could work out an arrangement in advance. Like, Rose could keep a few frozen pies on hand? Frozen pies were good, but freshly made pies were better and when it came to her baked goods, Rose was a perfectionist, so she was conflicted. As much as she needed the money, this wasn't a matter she could decide on the spot. "I—I would have to think about it and get back to you with an answer," she said.

Helen thanked her profusely for her consideration. Then she pointed to the wagon. "You must have pies in there—I can smell them. There's nothing stopping me from buying three or four of them today, is there?"

"*Neh*, of course not," Rose answered, and after the woman paid her, she helped load the pies into the trunk of her SUV. "I can let you know my decision tomorrow morning."

"I understand. You probably need to sleep on it, right?" Helen guessed. "Or is it that you have to talk it over with your husband first?"

Rather than informing the woman she wasn't married, Rose lifted her chin and said, "*Neh.* I don't need my husband's opinion, but I do need to pray about it. I'll be here at nine o'clock and we can talk then."

Because Caleb had spent Monday, Tuesday and Wednesday afternoons helping Rose pick berries, he'd had to complete several of his usual afternoon chores in the evening instead. Not that he regretted helping her, but it meant he hadn't been able to search the woods near the property after supper as he'd intended. On Thursday he'd had some spare time, but it was pouring outside and Caleb couldn't think of a convincing explanation for why he'd be walking around in the woods in that kind of weather, in the event someone saw him. Finally on Friday the rain tapered off and he seized the opportunity to go investigate the area while Rose, the girls and the guests were all in the dining hall serving and eating supper.

But it turned out the fern and undergrowth were so dense he had barely covered a hundred yards before he became discouraged, realizing that if a thief had buried something there in the spring, it would be covered completely with foliage by now. How was he going to tell Ryan about this? After another twenty minutes of plodding through the forest, Caleb gave up and turned around.

Tomorrow was a new day and he'd try again then. For now, his muscles ached and his mind was weary. If he were back in Wisconsin, he'd probably unwind by ordering a pizza and catching a Brewers game on TV, but tonight all Caleb wanted to do was to eat a big meal, take a shower, read the Bible and go to bed. It occurred to him he was becoming a little more like the Amish every day, and he hummed as he headed toward the dining hall for supper and a piece of Rose's pie.

Chapter Five

After praying and giving careful consideration to Helen's request, Rose decided she'd agree to make and set aside four extra pies for her daily, except on Sunday. This was in addition to the pies she'd put out on the stand for the general public. When she told her plan to Caleb and the girls at dinner on Friday night, Caleb sounded bewildered.

"But she's essentially a competitor," he said. "Wouldn't Sol and Nancy object to you helping her business?"

Like so many of Caleb's notions, this one struck Rose as odd. "How is she in competition with us? She runs a luxury *Englisch* inn on a busy lake. It's not as if our customers will suddenly choose to go there instead, simply because she serves my pies. My *ant* and *onkel* would be pleased someone else could benefit from the farm *Gott* blessed them with, and they'd be happy I could earn extra money, too."

Eleanor chimed in, "And if you think about it, she could just show up early at the produce stand every morning and buy the pies before anyone else gets there. At least this way Rose will get double the money."

"*Neh*, I won't," Rose said. "I've decided it wouldn't be right to charge her double."

Caleb seemed as nonplussed by this as Rose had been by his suggestion she shouldn't help Helen's business succeed. "It's not as if you're cheating her—she *offered* you double."

"*Neh*. A pie is a pie. The Lord despises unfair scales," she responded, loosely quoting the Biblical proverb. Rose couldn't fault Caleb and Eleanor's reasoning as she'd wavered about the issue herself, but in the end, she knew charging one customer more than her other customers wouldn't be pleasing to God.

When Rose told Helen on Saturday she'd make the pies but couldn't accept double payment, Helen seemed as puzzled as Caleb had appeared. She tried to persuade Rose to at least agree to what she called a "special order fee," but Rose held firm. She explained the other terms of their arrangement—that Helen or her staff would pick up the pies at the produce stand so as not to disturb the guests by coming to the dining hall. "And I'd appreciate your understanding if unusual circumstances prevent me from baking on rare occasion," Rose said.

"Of course," Helen chirped. When Rose extended her hand to shake on the deal, the way the *Englisch* did, Helen hugged her instead. Rose was surprised and pleased by the warm gesture.

Since it was Saturday, Rose's changeover chores kept her busy until almost four o'clock. She stole a moment to check on the raspberry bushes—it appeared some of them would be ready for harvesting next week—when she walked to the main road to retrieve the mail from its box. There were letters for the girls, as well as two for herself: one from Nancy and one from her mother.

She waited until she was seated at the desk in the hall to read them.

The letter from Rose's aunt began with a description of the landscape. *"I love the height of the trees in Maine but I'd forgotten how much I miss the wide-open farmland here in Ohio,"* her aunt wrote. Then she said Sol had completed his first week of treatment with few adverse side effects so far. *"*Gott *is good and we trust in His Providence."*

Her letter continued, *"As I wrote to Charity and Hope, I forgot to tell you we asked the deacon and his wife to worship with you on off-Sundays, so expect a visit from Abram and Jaala. I imagine you'll have plenty of leftovers to serve for lunch."*

Off-Sundays referred to every other Sabbath, when the Amish worshipped with their families at home instead of together as a congregation. Although Rose would have been perfectly comfortable worshipping with Hope, Charity and Caleb, she welcomed the opportunity to get to know Abram and Jaala better. Also, there was less chance Henry would come over and hang around for hours if the deacon was there.

Nancy ended with a postscript: *"How is Caleb working out? He seemed very nervous. I hope he feels at home and has settled in by now."* Recognizing her aunt's not-so-subtle reminder to be welcoming and patient toward Caleb, Rose chuckled. Nancy would be pleased to know how well they were getting along.

After refolding Nancy's letter and setting it aside to read again later, she slit open the envelope from her mother. She took a deep breath and began to read. *"Dear Rose,"* it said. *"This note probably finds you enjoying cool northern weather, but it is unseasonably hot and humid here. I noticed you didn't take either of your sweaters with you when you left, so if you need me to send them, let me know."*

Admittedly, a breeze off the lake kept the house relatively cool, but it was every bit as muggy in the fields here as it was in Pennsylvania, and Rose guffawed at her mother's offer. She had tried to convince Rose to pack warmer clothing before she'd left, but Rose had argued, "I'm only going to Maine, *Mamm*, not to the North Pole." Apparently, her mother still had her doubts.

Rose read on. *"Your father's gout is acting up again so he hasn't been able to walk, much less put on a boot to go to work. By the time you receive this, he should be better, Lord willing, but please remember him in your prayers."*

Rose felt a pinprick of guilt. She hadn't been praying consistently for her parents lately—her focus had been asking the Lord to heal her uncle and to help her earn the money she needed. She offered a silent prayer for her mother, father, siblings and their families before reading further. Her mother had devoted another paragraph to news about her brothers' carpentry business and her sisters' households.

In closing, she wrote, *"Baker came to visit on Tuesday. He told your father and me he felt terrible about what he did and that he's working three jobs in order to repay you sooner than he agreed. He seems truly repentant. If you've really forgiven him, you ought to reconsider him as a suitor, Rose. You wouldn't want to look back someday and regret not reconciling with him."*

"Ugh!" Rose didn't think she could possibly be more exasperated until she read her mother's final line: *"I gave him your address as he intends to write to you."*

Rose closed her eyes and shook her head. How could her mother do that to her? Obviously, she'd been taken in by Baker's smooth talking. Just like Rose had been once. She seethed. And what does she mean by "if you've really forgiven him"? Furthermore, how could her mother suggest she reconsider Baker as a suitor? Rose couldn't believe a mother would prefer her daughter to be courted by a man who'd behaved so duplicitously than to have her remain single. She felt sold out.

She slid a sheet of decorative paper from the desk drawer and inscribed, *"Dear Mother, Thank you for offering to send my sweater, but I am so hot here in Maine it's all I can do not to jump in the lake each afternoon!"*

I'm sorry to hear Dad has had gout again. I hope he remembered to use ice on his toe—last time that seemed to help him almost as much as the steroid shot he got from the doctor. I will continue praying for him and for all of you. The picnic you described sounded like fun. I wish I could have helped bake desserts. I also enjoyed hearing about Mary's new baby and I hope he continues to be a good sleeper.

I have *forgiven Baker but I wish you hadn't given him my address, as I don't want to enter into a correspondence—or a courtship—with him. However, I'm pleased to hear he intends to pay me back earlier than he agreed. If he does, I'll be able to repay the bank loan he caused me to default on sooner than expected, too.*

Rose paused. She'd deliberately included the phrase "he caused me to default on" to emphasize the consequences of Baker's actions, but her mother might see it as proof Rose hadn't genuinely forgiven him. She blotted it out and kept writing.

> *I've found a way to earn extra money so I'll be able to lease the café on Maple Street once it becomes available in the fall. I'm baking pies and selling jam.*

She wanted to add, *"So you needn't worry about my future as a single woman; I'll be fine on my own."* Instead, she requested her mother greet everyone for her and then she signed the letter, *"With love from Rose."*

Since it was past time to start supper for the guests, Rose put aside the stationery to write to her aunt later and flew down the path to the dining hall. Eleanor was already there for once and she'd prepped all the vegetables, so Rose had enough time to bake fresh pies for the new group of guests to eat for dessert. The pies were still warm when she served them à la mode, and the ice cream melted atop of the crust.

"Don't tell Nancy this, but that was the best strawberry-rhubarb pie I've ever eaten," one of the guests confided on his way out of the dining hall. According to Hope and Charity, the gruff old fisherman had been coming to the camp for five years, yet he rarely spoke a word to anyone.

"I'm glad you enjoyed it. The Lord *has* blessed us with a *wunderbaar* crop of strawberries this year," Rose answered modestly, although she couldn't have felt more tickled.

The moment was ruined when the fisherman clapped Caleb's shoulder before shuffling out the door and advising him, "You'd be wise to take good care of a wife who cooks and looks like yours does!"

Caleb is not *my husband and I* don't *need to be taken care of!* Fuming, Rose ducked out of the room.

As Rose disappeared into the kitchen, Caleb cringed. He understood the man intended to pay her a compliment, but even by *Englisch* standards, his remark was boorish. It was sexist. And by the way the nape of Rose's neck turned from tan to red, Caleb recognized how rankled she'd been by it. He wished he had spoken up in her defense, but it all happened so fast. Besides, what would he have said? *Rose isn't my wife, but I'm blessed to know her for reasons other than what she looks like or how she bakes?* That only would have embarrassed Rose more. *I'll have to speak to her about it in private*, he thought.

But when Rose returned to the dining hall with a tray of food for him and the others to eat, she was stone-faced, and he thought it better not to acknowledge the man's remark unless she brought it up.

As usual, Eleanor kept the conversation at the table going. "Caleb, you have *got* to see the fireworks on *Muundaag* evening."

"Fireworks?"

"*Jah.* It's the Fourth of July on *Muundaag.* A big group of us goes up to Serenity Ridge for the best view of the display. You'll join us, won't you?"

Caleb had been so involved in his responsibilities at the camp he'd lost track of the date and didn't realize it was almost July Fourth. During his summers with the family in Pennsylvania, Caleb learned the Amish didn't pledge allegiance to the flag because they considered their allegiance to be to God above all, but they were patriotic and enjoyed firework displays.

On one hand, he'd like to get away from the camp for a break, but if everyone else was going, staying behind would give him an opportunity to poke through the woods without being seen, especially if they left before dark. "Are you going, Rose?" he asked. Then he quickly added, "And you, too, Charity and Hope?"

"We're going with Miriam and her *breider, jah*," Charity said. "They're picking us up."

"*Neh*, I'm not going," Rose answered. "I have pies to bake in the early morning. The fireworks don't start until ten and it takes half an hour to get home from the ridge, so being out until eleven is too late for me."

No sense in me sticking around here, then. "That's too bad because it sounds like *schpass*," Caleb said. Then he told Eleanor and the twins, "I'll meet everyone there after I finish my evening chores."

"Getting to the ridge can be complicated, especially since the *Englisch* will be on the road, too, and we'll need to take the long way around," Eleanor said. "You're *wilkom* to *kumme* home with me when we're done serving supper. A couple of our friends are meeting Henry and me at our *haus* and then we're all traveling in the same buggy. We can bring you home afterward."

"I, uh, appreciate that, but I'm sure I can find the ridge myself. Rose will draw me a map, won't you, Rose?" One morning when Rose caught Caleb wandering through the woods near the field, he claimed he had no sense of direction, so she teasingly offered to draw him a map that showed how to get from the house to the garden. He made reference to her joke now, hoping to elicit a smile, but her expression and posture remained wooden.

"Jah," she agreed in a faraway voice.

The next morning Rose still seemed distracted as she, Hope and Charity sat with Caleb on the porch, waiting for Jaala and Abram. When they arrived, the six of them went inside and seated themselves in the gathering room. Since it was his first time this far inside the house, Caleb scanned his surroundings. This was the largest room in the house, but it was still small by Amish standards. Hope, Charity and Rose sat on the sofa and Jaala took the armchair, which Caleb noticed was the same type as those in the cabins. He and Abram sat in the straight-backed wooden chairs across from the women.

"Shall we pray?" Abram asked, and the women murmured their agreement. In the pause that followed, Rose touched her head and Caleb instantly realized she was signaling him to remove his hat. *I'm always forgetting to put it on or forgetting to take it off*, he thought sheepishly. As everyone else bowed their heads, Caleb mouthed *"denki"* to Rose, who nodded, her lips curving slightly before she bowed her head, too. If his embarrassment was the price of returning the smile to her face, Caleb was glad to pay it.

After singing hymns they knew by heart—fortunately, Caleb also remembered them from the Amish hymnal, the *Ausbund*—the deacon chose to read Colossians 3:1–14 from the Scriptures. The second verse especially captured Caleb's attention. It read, "Set your affection on things above, not on things on the earth," and reminded him of the text from the book of Matthew that was quoted in the note sent to Ryan. A chill swept up his spine. *The Bible is full of passages that echo or quote other passages,* he told himself. *It doesn't mean Abram knows anything about the note.*

Yet when the deacon read the first part of verse nine, which said, "Lie not one to another," Caleb would have claimed for certain Abram cleared his throat for emphasis; for condemnation. Or maybe that was Caleb's guilty conscience speaking.

He hadn't outright lied to anyone in Serenity Ridge, but he hadn't exactly been truthful, either. Prior to coming to the camp, Caleb had been concerned about being considered a fraud, being unfair to the Amish and possibly losing his job; now he was more concerned about how the Lord looked at what he was doing. Did the ends justify the means in God's sight? *But if I tell the Amish who I really am, I'll have to leave and my brother might lose his son...*

Hope's voice jarred Caleb from his conflicting thoughts. "The verse about setting our affections on things above, not on things on the earth reminds me of the sermon you gave this spring, Abram," Hope observed.

"*Jah*, me, too," Charity agreed.

The deacon beamed. "I'm glad you were listening so closely!"

He delivered a sermon on those verses earlier this spring? Caleb's pulse hammered his eardrums. *Is it possible the person who wrote the note is Amish?* Then his mind made an even bigger leap. *Could it have been Hope and Charity who wrote it? Or Nancy and Sol? Or...* No, Rose hadn't been at the camp when Ryan received the letter. It couldn't have been her. What if it was Abram himself?

"Caleb?" Obviously the deacon had asked him a question he hadn't heard.

"Excuse me?" Caleb felt the heat rising up his neck.

"I asked if you wanted to comment on any of the verses that struck a chord with you."

While everyone was waiting for him to say something, Caleb drew a blank. Now his ears were burning, as well as his neck and cheeks. He was grateful when Rose broke the silence.

"Verse 13, that part about forbearing and forgiving one another as Christ has forgiven us..." she began tentatively, her voice soft. "Sometimes I believe I've forgiven someone, but when I really consider my attitude toward them, I wonder if I've forgiven them as fully as *Gott* has forgiven me. Maybe I'm holding on to a little grudge."

"I understand what you mean," Jaala said. "We can pray about that for you—and for each other."

All Caleb could think was, *Who hasn't she forgiven completely? The guest from last night?* If she had difficulty forgiving a stranger for his impropriety, how would Rose ever forgive Caleb for masquerading as an Amish person?

He continued to fret as Abram led them in prayer and then in a few contemporary church songs. By the time they finished worshipping, it was almost noon, but for once, Caleb didn't feel hungry. His insides coiled into a tight lump, but he knew it would be rude not to eat with the others. Afterward he would go out on the lake by himself, he decided. He couldn't keep up this charade. He needed to find the coins and leave as soon as possible.

But while he and Abram were sitting on the porch waiting for the women to prepare lunch, the deacon suggested, "Let's take the canoe out to do a little fishing after we eat. Might not be the best time of day for it, but as long as I'm here…" And Caleb knew he couldn't refuse.

Rose was glad when Sunday was over. The Scripture had left her unsettled about whether she'd truly forgiven Baker. Forgiving him and accepting him as her suitor again were two different things, weren't they? *But I told* Mamm *I didn't even want to enter into a correspondence with him. If I'm really not harboring any ill will, why do I resent the idea of him writing to me?* Rose's thoughts vacillated so much she couldn't wait to get up and make pies on Monday. Sometimes it was easier to *do* than to think, and Rose's work was particularly rewarding that morning because Helen was delighted she was baking on the holiday.

Since the raspberries weren't quite ready for picking yet, Rose spent the afternoon putting up vegetables and making jam until it was almost suppertime. Most of the camp guests were either eating in restaurants or they were having Independence Day cookouts on Black Bear Lake, so preparing the evening meal for the few still at the camp was a cinch. For the staff's supper, Rose and Eleanor baked the trout Caleb caught the day before when he was fishing with Abram.

"This is *appenditlich*," Charity enthused when they'd finished their meal. "You should catch supper more often, Caleb."

"*Jah*, I wish *Daed* were here to go fishing with you. He loves being on the lake," Hope said wistfully. "Maybe if he's strong enough when he gets home, you two can go then."

"I'm sure he'll be well by summer's end," Caleb replied, nodding, yet somehow his reassurance was less than convincing.

Rose sighed. This wasn't the first comment the twins made that indicated how worried they were about their father's health. Hoping to cheer them, she instructed, "Okay, you'd all better get going. I'll take care of the cleanup tonight. Have *schpass* and be careful."

When she finished washing, drying and putting away the dishes, Rose removed the last of the rhubarb from the freezer to defrost it, and then she washed, hulled and cut strawberries. The process was becoming so familiar she imagined she could do it with her eyes closed; yet, she didn't seem to be getting any faster at it. It was almost nine when she finished and stepped outside into the near dark. The camp was unusually quiet, not a single guest on the property, and as she neared the main house, Rose was startled by a flickering movement ahead of her. *I have to quit this foolishness*, she thought. *I'm fine. Nothing's here.*

But as she set her foot on the bottom stair of the porch, she realized something definitely *was* there: a small and dark animal stood near the front door. A cat. But what was with it? Kittens? Then she recognized the telltale white stripe—it was a mother skunk with a surfeit of kits! There was just enough light for Rose to see the animal lift its tale, so she quietly and rapidly backed away before the creature became more agitated.

Now what was she going to do? she wondered from a safe distance. She had locked the back door and the basement hatchway, on Caleb's advice, and she didn't think she could climb into one of the first-story windows. It seemed her only option was to return to the dining hall and wait for the skunks to leave. After fifteen minutes, she crept toward the house and found they were still there. She left and came back a second time, but they appeared to have taken up permanent residence on the porch, so Rose decided this time she'd wait near the lake.

I would have been better off going to the fireworks display. The thought inspired her; although the hill of trees on the opposite shoreline would obscure the fireworks from view here, if she went to Paradise Point, she'd be able to see into the valley on the other side. *Why not? It's not as if I can go to bed anyway.*

In addition to a life vest, Rose retrieved a flashlight from the nearby storage shed. As she was flipping the canoe right side up, Rose distinctly heard footfalls on the path and she held her breath. It had to be a moose or a deer; no one else was at the camp. Or could it be a bear? Reflexively she picked up the canoe paddle and raised it over her head, hoping it would make her appear bigger, which in turn might frighten an animal away. "Who's there?" she shouted, just as something stepped into the clearing by the water.

"Don't swing!" a man warned. "It's me, Caleb."

"You scared me!" she scolded, lowering the paddle. "What are you doing here?"

"I thought I heard something, so I came to see what it was."

"*Neh*, I meant what are you doing back already? The fireworks haven't even begun yet."

"Well, someone agreed to draw a map for me and she forgot, and I didn't want to disturb her since I figured she was intent on making pies..."

"Oh, *neh*! I'm sorry. You should have asked me again."

"I was kidding. Actually, I got about halfway there and ran into a huge traffic jam, and since I'm pretty bushed anyway, I decided it wasn't worth the effort. What are *you* doing down here at this hour?"

Rose explained the skunk situation and couldn't resist needling him. "I blame you for this, you know. I never would have locked the back door and hatchway if you hadn't made such a *schtinke* about our safety."

"I'd say I'm sorry but I'm not. I still think it's for the best that you lock up."

"Jah, jah," Rose grumbled good-naturedly. "Anyway, I was just about to go up to Paradise Point to watch the fireworks from there."

"Alone? In the dark?"

"I have a flashlight." She shone it in his face, and he swatted at the ray of light as if it was a bug until she turned it off.

"Do you mind if I *kumme* with you?"

"You just said you were tired."

"*Jah*, but I'd feel personally responsible if anything happened to you," he said. "Or to anyone who crosses your path."

"Voll schpass." She laughed. "Okay, but hurry up—and wear your boots."

As they paddled across the lake, Rose pointed out the fireflies blinking brightly beneath the trees along the shoreline. "Look. Our own private fireworks display."

"And the best thing is they're *silent* fireworks."

"You don't like how noisy fireworks are?"

"Let's just say I've really *kumme* to appreciate the serenity of Serenity Lake."

"Isn't it quiet where you live in Wisconsin?"

"It's not *this* quiet. This peaceful. There's something about being here, where sometimes the loudest sound I hear is water lapping the shore… It makes me feel so calm. I feel like that when I'm working in the fields, too. Probably because when I was young I used to escape to the garden when—"

Rose stopped paddling, eager to hear the rest of his sentence. He hardly ever talked about his youth. "When what?" she pressed, looking over her shoulder to get a glimpse of his face.

Over the past couple of weeks while chatting with Rose, Caleb had occasionally forgotten to guard his *Englisch* identity, but until now, he'd always guarded his emotions, especially those concerning his upbringing. He hadn't meant to disclose his feelings tonight—he hadn't even intended to spend any time alone with Rose. But opening up to her seemed to happen naturally, in spite of yesterday's resolution to put distance between himself and the Amish of Serenity Ridge. So he continued, "My *mamm* and *daed* bickered a lot and it helped to go outdoors to get away from them. When I was gardening, I forgot about their troubles. Tending to *Gott*'s creation made me feel… Well, it made me feel tranquil." *Kind of like how I feel right now.*

Caleb had also stopped paddling and mild waves gently rocked the canoe. In the moonlight, he could see Rose's eyebrows were furrowed and she appeared to be contemplating what he'd just said. After a quiet spell, she questioned, "Does gardening still bring you a sense of tranquility?"

"*Jah*, it does." Caleb's mouth went dry as he anticipated her next question: she was going to ask why he'd become a teacher instead of a farmer, and he couldn't drum up a credible reply.

Instead, she gave him a fetching smile and, before

twisting forward in her seat again, she added, "I'm glad. For our sake, as well as for yours."

Caleb let his breath out slowly. He dipped his paddle into the water and Rose did, too. As they journeyed he thought about how amazing it felt to confide in her. Maybe he wasn't being honest about the facts of his life, but tonight he'd been honest about his emotions. And even though Rose's back was to him as she sat in the bow, there was something so…not necessarily *romantic*, but so *personal* about being with her that he'd never felt with his friends or any of the women he'd ever dated. *Rose seems to enjoy spending time with me, too,* Caleb rationalized. *So what's the harm in continuing to develop friendships here as long as no one finds out I'm* Englisch*?*

When they pulled onto the shore near the trailhead by Paradise Point, Caleb hopped out and dragged the canoe several feet up the embankment so Rose wouldn't get her shoes wet, and then they headed for the forested path. It was much darker beneath the trees than on the open water, so Rose shone the flashlight on the ground in front of her. Caleb initially tried to follow in her footsteps but after tripping twice, he decided to accompany her side by side on the narrow path in order to get the benefit of the light.

"I think we should talk so we don't startle any animals," Rose announced loudly. "Or we should sing."

"My singing *would* frighten the animals," Caleb jested.

"In that case, you should have serenaded the skunks on the porch—maybe they would have left."

"Or they would have sprayed me," Caleb said. "This probably isn't the right time to ask, but are there many other kinds of animals in these woods?"

"Serenity Ridge has a family of moose that sometimes make their presence known. The other night when I was coming back from the dining hall, I thought I heard one in the bushes behind me, but then it went quiet."

Caleb's ears perked up. "What night was that?"

"I think it was last Monday or Tuesday, but don't worry, it turned out to be a deer—I saw its tracks on the path. That's the thing about animals and *buwe*—they always leave tracks. When my *breider* were young, my *mamm* always knew when they'd been exploring down by the swamp instead of doing their chores because of what her kitchen floor looked like. You'd think it would occur to them to take off their shoes before they came inside, but it never did," Rose said, giggling.

For the rest of their hike Caleb asked questions about her siblings and their families, and he told her a couple anecdotes about Ryan, too. Finally the trees thinned out and Rose announced they were nearing the summit. Caleb was about to remark he wished they'd brought refreshments when he heard a noise in the distance, almost a metallic sound, or like something scraping against a rock. He came to a halt and tugged Rose's arm to make her stop, too. With his chin nearly resting on her shoulder, he whispered into her ear, "What was that?"

"I didn't hear anything," she whispered back, and flashed the light into the woods on one side of the path and then the other. Caleb didn't see anything unusual. He didn't hear anything unusual, either, other than the thundering of his pulse, which was probably more from standing so close to Rose than from being alarmed. Half a minute passed and nothing stirred in the woods.

He must have imagined it, Caleb thought, merely two seconds before an earsplitting shot reverberated through the night air.

Chapter Six

Rose giggled when Caleb nearly leaped out of his skin—he was even jumpier than she'd been lately. "Quick, they're starting the fireworks!" she exclaimed as a volley of initial explosions resonated in the valley. She hurried the last few yards up the wooded path into the clearing. From there they'd have to scramble up a gravelly incline in order to gain enough height to see beyond the trees, but they wouldn't have enough time or light to scale the larger rocks comprising the ridge. "It's treacherous up here. Don't trip."

A few more separate booms sounded as Rose led Caleb to a rounded boulder. They hoisted themselves onto it right before the sky erupted into a dazzling kaleidoscopic array of designs and the accompanying cacophony ricocheted off the surrounding ridges and hills. Rose nudged Caleb and pointed to the lake below, which reflected splendorous patterns flaring across the sky.

"It's doubly beautiful," he mumbled—exactly what she'd been thinking.

Rose glanced at his profile, which was illuminated by the prismatic flickering of the exploding fireworks. He'd removed his hat, and his head was tilted slightly upward, damp curls sticking to his forehead and temples. He was slack jawed and motionless except for the occasional lowering and lifting of the long dark fringe of his eyelashes. Rose was nearly as mesmerized by his astonishment as he was by the fireworks, and she had to force her gaze back toward the sky.

"Ooh," she sighed, touching her throat as resplendence shattered the dark.

"Ahh," Caleb exclaimed after a particularly radiant shower of color rained down from above.

When neon green, yellow and purple streaks zigzagged through the night, simultaneously they said, "Wow." Then they looked at each other and burst out laughing. Rose didn't know what was so funny, but she couldn't contain her glee. And when the grand finale rocketed through the atmosphere with chromatic explosions too spectacular for words, they hopped to their feet and applauded while vehicles in the distant valley honked their horns. As it quieted, Rose and Caleb stood shoulder to shoulder, watching the cloud of smoke drift over the far hills.

"That was..." Caleb appeared to be searching for a word.

Rose understood without him saying it. "*Jah*, it was." She pushed the button on her flashlight, which cast a feeble glow. She shook it and smacked it against her palm, but the light remained dim.

"Here, let me try." Caleb unscrewed the top, took the batteries out and reinserted them; this time the light wouldn't come on. "We'll just have to take it slowly. Let me go first," he said. He made his way down the incline sideways, bracing his forearm at a perpendicular angle so Rose could lean on it for balance. As she did, she thought of Julia. Rose supposed if someone saw her and Caleb just now they might jump to conclusions similar to those she'd been afraid they'd make about Caleb escorting Julia to her car. *I hope we get back to the camp before the* Englischers *do*, she fretted. *I don't want to give anyone the wrong impression.*

When they reached the beginning of the path through the woods, Rose released her grip, but at that second something flapped erratically between the trees. She screamed and grabbed Caleb's arm with one hand, using her other hand to cover her head.

"It was just a bat," he informed her.

"Ick!" Rose crouched lower.

"How can someone who doesn't sleep with her doors locked and who's willing to hike up a mountain in the dark alone be afraid of bats?"

"I'm not *afraid* of them." Rose burrowed her face into her arm. "I just don't like them swooping at my head."

"You know it's a myth that they make nests in women's hair, right?"

"*Jah*. So?"

"And they won't bump into you by accident. They use echolocation and they can catch insects midair, so they have really good aim," he reasoned.

"They also have rabies," she said, peeking over her elbow at him. "Some of them do anyway."

"Well, you've seen what happened to the canoe when you tried traveling blindfolded, so you can't walk down the trail with your eyes covered." Rose understood Caleb was trying to quell her anxiety with humor, but it wasn't working: she really, really loathed bats. "Do you want to wear my *hut*? You can keep the brim lowered so you won't notice them."

"*Them?* There's more than one?" she whimpered.

Caleb pried her fingers from his arm and tugged her hand from her head so he could place his hat on her. Even atop of her prayer *kapp*, the hat wiggled loosely, and as Rose tilted her head to look at him, the brim slipped forward, reducing her vision. "I can hardly see."

"That's the point. You keep looking down at your feet while I lead you forward," he said definitively, clasping her hand in his.

"But it's dark. How will *you* see?"

"I'll manage."

"We're going to go back the same way we came up, right? Because you don't know the way on the other paths and they're difficult to follow even during the day."

"*Jah.* We're going back the same way we came up," he assured her. "Ready?"

Rose took a deep breath. "Ready."

Although she was nervously chatting nonstop, after a few minutes Rose loosened her grip so her fingertips weren't pressing into the back of Caleb's hand. *If only she weren't so anxious...* Then what? She might enjoy walking hand in hand with him? Caleb quickly dismissed the thought, reminding himself that she wasn't holding his hand because she wanted to.

The difficulty of navigating through the dark, combined with Rose's halting pace, made for a slow descent and it probably took them twice as long as usual to get to the end of the trail. "We're almost to the bottom," Caleb told Rose. "Finally."

"Sorry I was so slow. You must really regret not going to Serenity Ridge instead."

"Not at all," he answered honestly as he led her into the clearing. "This has been much more—hey! Where's the canoe?" It wasn't resting where he'd left it on the embankment.

Rose dropped his hand and lifted the hat from her head. "What in the world…? Oh, look, there it is, over there." The boat was floating to the west, some twenty yards from shore.

"How did that happen? Is this a prank?"

"Neh," Rose assured him. "It must have drifted off. We probably didn't pull it out of the water far enough."

Caleb was already taking off his boots. "I made sure it was secure. Those tiny waves couldn't have carried it away—a person had to have moved it." He unlaced his other boot.

"But there weren't any other boats here when we came. And no one can access Paradise Point from the other side—it's private property."

"That doesn't mean it can't be accessed. Besides, someone might have *kumme* here after we started hiking."

"Maybe," Rose said. "But who would do that?"

Who, indeed? "I'll be right back." Caleb waded into the chilly water until it reached his waist, and then he dived forward and swam to retrieve the canoe, tugging it to shore by its rope.

"*Denki* for doing that," she said. "You must be cold."

"Neh," he said. "Just wet."

"At least your hat is dry." Rose pointed to her head.

"My boots are, too." Caleb picked up his footwear and held the canoe steady for Rose to climb in. They both donned their life vests and then he pushed off from shore.

"*Now* are you sorry you didn't go to Serenity Ridge instead?" she asked as they paddled across the lake.

"Neh," he answered. "Aside from almost getting clobbered with a paddle and going for a midnight swim in my clothes, this has been the most *schpass* I've had in ages. I didn't even mind your tantrum about the bats."

"I'd splash you for that, but you're already wet so it wouldn't do any *gut*."

"With the way things are going tonight, we'd probably capsize," Caleb said, chuckling. *Yet even if we did, I'd still choose hanging out with you over being anywhere else.*

When they pulled ashore, Rose was relieved to see all the cabins were dark—undoubtedly the guests had already returned and were in bed. Not wishing to wake them or be seen coming home with Caleb, she whispered, "Look, a light is on at the *haus*. That means the *meed* must have gotten home and the skunks are gone."

"*Gut*—otherwise I would have had to pop a screen and boost one of you through a window."

Rose realized she was actually glad he hadn't thought of that earlier, because she would have missed out on an adventurous evening. They flipped the canoe on the sand, and put the paddles and life vests in the shed. Just as they reached the fork in the path veering off to his cabin, a bright light shone in their eyes.

"Rose? Caleb?" Charity questioned loudly. "Are you okay? Where have you been?"

"Shh, you'll wake the guests," Rose scolded. Suddenly Hope stepped forward and threw her arms around

Rose, sobbing audibly into her neck. "What's wrong, Hope? *Kumme* to the *haus* and we'll talk about it there."

Rose's heart drummed her ribs as the four of them hurried toward the house. Had the girls received news about Sol? *Please, Lord, show me how to comfort them*, she prayed desperately. Or had something happened that upset them at the fireworks? Maybe Oliver Graham had said something to them again…

Once they were in the gathering room, Hope sank into the couch and covered her eyes with her arm, much like Rose had after seeing the bats. Rose settled beside her and placed a hand on the middle of her shoulders while Charity paced across the rag rug in the center of the room. Caleb, still wet, stood in the doorway.

"What's wrong? Why are you crying?" Rose asked at the same time Charity questioned if Rose and Caleb had capsized on the lake.

"*Neh*, we're fine. You tell us what's wrong, first," Rose insisted.

Charity explained, "Caleb never showed up to the fireworks, and when we got home you weren't here, either, Rose. We didn't know what happened to you. We waited and waited. Hope recalled what Oliver Graham said about the thief, and the longer we waited the more worried we got. I thought Hope was going to hyperventilate. Why didn't you leave a note?"

"Oh, Hope," Rose moaned, patting her back. "I'm so sorry I gave you such a fright—both of you. A skunk and her kits were on the porch so I couldn't get into the *haus* to leave you a note. I thought I'd be home long before you got here."

"I'm sorry, too," Caleb said. "There was a traffic jam so I decided not to go to the ridge after all. Rose wanted to see the fireworks from Paradise Point and I didn't think it was *schmaert* for her to go alone, so I went with her. Somehow our canoe floated off and I had to swim after it. Otherwise, we would have been back before you were."

Rose was grateful he didn't tell the girls her disdain for bats had caused an additional delay. "I really didn't mean to worry you," she repeated, leaning closer to take Hope's hand from her eyes.

"Well, you *did*," Charity said accusingly before slumping into the armchair. She muttered, "*We're* the teenagers. The two of you are supposed to worry about us, not the other way around."

Rose chuckled, glad the tension was dissipating. "We promise not to do anything that will make you worry in the future, okay? But I can see we're all letting our imaginations run away with us. We never worried about criminals harming us before, and we don't need to worry about them now. And I think we ought to leave the back door unlocked during the day like we used to, so this kind of thing doesn't happen again. Especially with the skunks coming up on the porch."

As remorseful as he was the girls had suffered such distress, Caleb didn't agree that they should leave the back door unlocked. "I'll put something out to deter the skunks from coming around, so it's fine to keep the back door locked," he suggested lightly, hoping to change Rose's mind about locking up.

"As long as you use something natural that won't harm our guests or their children, I'd appreciate that," Rose said, but she didn't commit to keeping the back door locked. "Speaking of our guests, we'd better get to bed so we can be up in time to make them breakfast tomorrow."

Caleb bade the women good-night and walked down the path, shaking his clothes so they wouldn't cling to his skin when he moved. Once inside the cabin, he reached to take a dry change of clothes from his dresser and noticed the drawer wasn't closed all the way. *That's odd. I'm usually careful because that's the drawer I keep my cell phone in*, he thought and immediately pulled the drawer open. But no, his cell phone was beneath a stack of socks, right where he had left it. *Maybe Rose is right—maybe I'm being paranoid*, he thought as he rubbed his head dry with a towel.

Stretching out in bed a few minutes later, he reflected on the chaotic evening. Despite the minor calamities, Caleb felt oddly sedate and when sleep carried him away, he dreamed about fireflies and fireworks.

The next morning over breakfast, Charity commented, "Was the view worth the climb up to Paradise Point last night, Caleb and Rose?"

"Absolutely," she replied without hesitation.

At the same time, Caleb answered, "*Jah*, it sure was."

Eleanor glanced at him and then at Rose and then back at him before complaining, "You should have been honest from the start, Caleb. If you didn't want to *kumme* to the ridge, you should have told me and I wouldn't have wasted my time looking out for you."

"I *was* being honest," Caleb protested. "But there must have been an accident because there was a huge traffic jam, so I came back. Rose just happened to—"

"You don't need to explain. I won't tell the deacon." Eleanor stuck her chin in the air.

"Tell the deacon what?"

"That you and Rose are courting."

"We are not!" Rose and Caleb said, again in unison.

Then Rose added, "Even if we were, it wouldn't be anyone else's business and I don't see why the deacon would care."

"Because you hardly know each other. And what would the *Englischers* have thought if they'd seen you sneaking back from Paradise Point in the dark? It's unseemly."

Caleb was indignant. "I'd never do anything to jeopardize Rose's reputation. Or mine."

Rose stood up and declared, "We haven't been *sneaking* anywhere!" She pushed her chair back and went into the kitchen.

"What's she so angry about? I said I *wasn't* going to tell the deacon. I didn't say I *was*," Eleanor grumbled, her cheeks pink.

The twins looked down at their plates and quickly gobbled their food. Caleb no longer felt hungry. "I've got some skunks to track down," he said and strode out the door.

Does anyone else think Rose and I are courting? Or, worse, did anyone think they were "sneaking around," or otherwise acting inappropriately, as Eleanor suggested? Caleb didn't want a rumor like that getting back to Nancy and Sol—they might worry Caleb and Rose weren't setting a good example for the twins. He couldn't let that happen. As much as he resented it, Caleb once again decided it was in everyone's best interest if he spent less time with Rose.

It was probably just as well. Searching for the family of skunks provided him a unique opportunity to look for the coins, too. Skunks frequently nested beneath porches, in hollow logs and even in patches of vegetation in warmer weather. So Caleb had the perfect excuse for poking around the property again and searching the woods without arousing suspicion.

After placing citrus peels around the perimeter of the main house to prevent the skunks from returning to the porch, Caleb set out to scrutinize the forested area on both sides of the camp. But after a week of looking, he hadn't discovered any trace of the smelly little critters or of the artifacts. He'd hardly seen hide nor hair of Rose, either, except at mealtimes. At first he figured her raspberry picking and pie making was keeping her as busy as he was, but after a while he began to wonder if she was more intimidated by Eleanor's comment than she'd let on. Was it possible she was as concerned about her immature coworker spreading rumors as Caleb was? If so, then she probably appreciated him keeping his distance.

However, by Saturday he was so restless and irritable from prohibiting himself from socializing with her, Caleb called Ryan an hour early, even though he had no news to report. No good news anyway. "I've been foraging through the woods all week. Granted, the overgrowth is awfully thick, but I haven't come across anything that looks remotely like something's buried or hidden there."

Ryan sighed so heavily into the phone it sounded like a rush of wind. "Well," he said after a pause, "I appreciate it that you're still trying."

"Don't lose heart. I haven't even begun to search the islands or the places where the Amish are allowed to hike. I'll do that tomorrow after church, since that's when I can use the canoe," he said, trying to encourage his brother. "So, how is Liam doing?"

"Not great. I think he picked up a virus from the pool. And whenever he's sick, he wants Sheryl to take care of him, so I won't get to see him this weekend."

Caleb heard the note of loneliness in his brother's voice, and as he surveyed the glittering lake and felt the soft current blowing through his window he wished he could invite Ryan to Serenity Ridge for a while. The lake would do him good. "That's got to be—"

Rose's sudden appearance at his door caught him off guard; Caleb had completely forgotten to close up the cabin before making his call. He disconnected, but it was too late.

"Who are you talking to?" she asked, peering through the screen.

"I—I—I..." He couldn't think of an answer quickly enough and if he tried to hide his phone, he'd only draw more attention to it. He held it up for her to see and stepped outside. "I called my *bruder*."

"You own a cell phone? I've never heard of an Old Order *Ordnung* that allows the Amish to use cell phones for personal calls," she commented, pinching her brows together. Before he could respond, she added, "But then again, I'd never heard of Old Order Amish men being allowed to wear mustaches until I came to Maine, either."

"*Jah*, the mustaches men wear with their beards here surprised me, too," Caleb agreed. Although he felt guilty for not contradicting the conclusion Rose had made about his cell phone use, he was relieved she didn't quiz him further on it. He added, "I only use this to talk about urgent matters with my *bruder* while I'm away."

"Is there an emergency?" she asked, and the lines of

concern etched across her forehead made Caleb wish he'd shut his mouth while he was ahead.

"*Neh*, but his *suh* is ill, so I was, uh, just checking in..." Yes, Liam was ill, but it wasn't his illness that had prompted Caleb's call, and he felt ashamed for implying it was. "He's getting better, though. Anyway, are those for me?"

"Jah." She extended a stack of folded sheets. "Before Hope and Charity went out they mentioned they forgot to drop these off today."

"Denki." The back of Caleb's hand grazed her arm as he took the linens, and her smooth skin made him shiver. "I also came to invite you up to the porch for a piece of *aebeer hembeer boi.* I'm experimenting with the recipe and I need your expert opinion."

"I, uh... *Denki*, but my stomach is a little off, so I'll have to pass," he said, which was true; misleading Rose was making Caleb feel sick.

Rose wished she could fly away like the swallow she spied from the corner of her eye. At least, she *hoped* it was a swallow. She managed to squeak, "Oh, okay. I'll see you tomorrow for *kurrich.*" Then she beat a path to the main house. *He's never refused food before, especially pie. I wonder if he's still embarrassed by what Eleanor said about what the* Englischers *might think if they saw us together. Especially since some of them already think we're married...*

Rose had been concerned about that herself, even before Eleanor opened her big mouth, but that was why she'd intended to visit with Caleb on the porch in plain view before the sun set. It was also why she'd allowed nearly a week to pass without so much as crossing his path when she saw him outdoors. She wanted to prove to Eleanor—and to anyone else—there was absolutely nothing going on between them. Besides, raspberry picking kept her occupied and Caleb seemed to be on a perpetual hunt for the skunks, wolfing down his meals and then running off to the woods. However, after five or six days of barely speaking an extra word to each other, Rose had hoped he'd be as eager to catch up with her as she was to chat with him. She was crushed he'd turned down her invitation.

Now what am I going to do tonight? Charity and Hope were helping Miriam bake a cake for her brother's birthday on Sunday, so Rose was stuck home alone with nothing to keep her company except the letter she'd received that afternoon from Baker. *I might as well read it*, she silently conceded.

After serving herself a big slice of pie—*Caleb's loss is my gain*—she carried the dessert and letter to the porch and settled into a glider. She took a bite and allowed it to dissolve on her tongue. Then another. Nope, too sweet. She shouldn't have added that extra tablespoon of sugar. She opened the envelope and removed Baker's letter.

"Dear Rosie," he'd written, using his nickname for her as if they were still courting. She was already annoyed and she hadn't even made it past the salutation! *"Your mother gave me your address so I could send the enclosed money order for twice what I owe you."*

"It's not twice what you owe me," Rose said aloud. "It's a *fraction* of what you owe me. It's just two installments paid at the same time."

Don't worry, I haven't been selling horses again, just training them. I've also taken an eve-

ning and Saturday job at Detweiler's hardware store. I hope this shows how sincere I am about earning back your trust so things can go back to how they were between us.

Rose threw her hand in the air and brought it down against her thigh with a slap. Baker was mistaking earning money with earning trust. Repaying a debt wasn't the same thing as reconciling a relationship. It was as if he thought her trust could be *bought.* As if it were a simple financial transaction.

Do you go canoeing often at Serenity Lake? Remember when we rowed across the reservoir? I think of that often.
Yours,
Baker.

"Ugh!" Rose crumpled the letter into a ball. Yes, she remembered when they went out on the reservoir in a rowboat. It was where they first kissed. At the time, she'd found it very romantic, but it bothered her that Baker thought about that part of their past. She certainly didn't. And she didn't think about a future with him, either. She'd told him as much when she broke up with him. Why wasn't it sinking in? Did he think with time she'd change her mind?

When she returned to Pennsylvania, Rose was going to have to disavow him, for once and for all, of the notion she'd ever accept him back as a suitor. For now, though, Rose was going to savor her pie and the view. Alone. Without Baker, without Caleb. And that was just fine by her.

* * *

Caleb regretted declining Rose's invitation to join him for a slice of pie; not only did his stomach settle down a few minutes after she left, but he missed hanging out with her. More important, he sensed she felt slighted by his rejection of the offer. Hurting Rose's feelings was exactly the opposite of what Caleb intended by turning her down, and he stayed awake most of the night wrestling with his conscience. Shortly before the sun came up, he concluded he'd do more harm than good by continuing to steer clear of her. And as for Eleanor or anyone else gossiping about him and Rose… Well, Caleb would be careful not to do anything to give them that impression. Or at least, he wouldn't go off with Rose after dark again. *But I sure could use her guidance on the side trails at Paradise Point, since she said they were difficult to follow.*

So, the next day after church when the twins left with their friends and Caleb was riding home alone with Rose, he asked if she'd like to go hiking to the Point when they got back.

Rose hesitated before answering. "*Jah*, okay. If you anticipate we'll be gone awhile, I'll pack a light supper, but I'd like to be home before dark."

Either she didn't want to meet up with bats again or else she had the same qualms he had about what Eleanor said. Either way, it didn't matter; they'd be home long before the sun set. Caleb hadn't realized until just then how much he'd missed hanging out with Rose, and he bit his lip to keep from whistling.

"I saw you in the woods a couple times this week," she remarked a little farther down the road. "Was your search successful? Did you find them?"

Caleb's head jerked backward in alarm. *She can't possibly know about the coins!* "Find what?" he stalled.

"The skunks. Or their nest."

His heart resumed beating and Caleb blew air from his cheeks. "*Neh.* I'm going to keep looking, though."

When they arrived at the barn, he stayed behind to unhitch the buggy while Rose dashed off to change her clothes and fill a small cooler with food. They agreed to meet down by the lake, but as Caleb was pulling the life vests from the shed, he glanced toward the main house and noticed a small group of Amish visitors gathered on the porch. One of them—it appeared to be the deacon—waved. Waving back, Caleb groaned. *Not today! It's the first time I've been alone with Rose in a week, and it's the only day I can search the trails.*

Within moments, Abram and two other men traipsed down the hill carrying fishing equipment. Caleb recognized Levi Swarey, who owned a Christmas tree farm, and Abram introduced Caleb to the younger man, a carpenter named Isaiah Gerhart.

"Hello, Caleb," the deacon greeted him. "We figured you could use some male companionship for a change."

Why? Did Eleanor tell Abram I've been spending a lot of time with Rose, or is he saying that because I'm the only Amish man at the camp? Caleb forced a grin and said he was glad they'd come. After he'd distributed life vests and gathered fishing equipment for himself from the shed, Caleb climbed into a canoe with Isaiah. As the foursome paddled onto the lake, Levi commented, "I can still hear the *bobbel* crying from here."

"Levi and his wife, Sadie, have a newborn. A *maedel*," Abram explained. "So he's on high alert."

"Sadie says I worry more about little Susannah than she does," Levi admitted.

Caleb asked Isaiah, "Is the other woman I saw on the porch your wife?"

"*Neh.* That's Irene Larson," he answered curtly. Then Caleb realized of course she wasn't his wife; Isaiah was clean-shaven.

Caleb immediately tried to compensate for his error. "I meant to ask if she's your girlfriend."

This time Isaiah didn't answer at all and the other men acted as if he hadn't spoken, too. *Ach! Now I've come across as being as nosy as Eleanor*, Caleb realized.

Later, when there was more distance between the two canoes, Caleb quietly apologized for being intrusive. "Sorry about asking you about Irene back there. In my, uh… In Wisconsin we're not as discreet about our courtships as people are here. I didn't mean to put you on the spot—especially in front of the deacon."

Isaiah chuckled. "I think Abram was more shocked by your question than I was. You see, Irene's *Englisch.*"

Caleb was floored. "But she was wearing Amish clothing!"

"*Jah.* That's because she's going through the convincement process to become Amish. The *kurrich* recently voted to accept her and she'll be baptized in the fall."

"Aha." Now Caleb understood: the Amish were strictly prohibited from dating *Englischers*, and until Irene was baptized, she was considered to be *Englisch.* So even if Isaiah was interested in Irene romantically, he could never let on. *Kind of like if Rose were interested in me*, Caleb thought before quickly dismissing the unbidden comparison.

"Irene's one of three *Englischers* who will be baptized this fall."

"Three?" Successful *Englisch*-to-Amish conversions were very rare, so three at once seemed like a high number to Caleb.

"Because our community here is small and relatively isolated, our district is more open to *Englischers* joining us than they are, say, in central Pennsylvania."

Why this information should fill Caleb with hope he wasn't sure, because it wasn't as if *he* could permanently join Serenity Ridge's Amish community, not after deceiving them the way he'd been doing. But he felt buoyed by the conversation all the same. In fact, Caleb enjoyed the long afternoon on the lake with the other men far more than he expected to, even though he didn't get to look for the coins or spend time with Rose.

It was close to six o'clock when the four men approached the porch, where Sadie was beckoning her twins, Elizabeth and David, to come inside for supper. Everyone took turns washing their hands in the bathroom. Caleb was the last to enter the kitchen, and as he scanned the table for an empty seat, his eye settled on Rose. Sitting near the far end of the table, she was cooing to baby Susannah as she cradled her in the crook of her arm.

Rose appeared as striking and strong as she had the first day Caleb spotted her paddling on the lake. But instead of scowling at him now as she'd done then, when Rose glanced up she smiled. It was enough to take Caleb's breath away and he was certain the deacon heard him gasp, so he quickly covered his mouth and coughed, as if something had tickled his throat instead of his heart.

Chapter Seven

"I can take the *bobbel* now, Rose," Sadie offered after the deacon said grace.

"That's okay. You probably never get to use both of your hands during your meal." Rose sniffed the dark, wispy hair on the chubby baby's head. "She's so sweet. If she were mine I don't think I'd ever put her down."

"You would if you knew how much her *windel schtinke*," eight-year-old David said, plugging his nose and waving his hand in front of his face.

"Mind your manners, *suh*," Levi reminded the child gently, but everyone else cracked up.

"Talk about *schtinke*, the other night I had a *familye* of skunks on my front porch." Rose delved into the story of how the creatures had blocked her from entering the house. She left out the parts that might be scary, such as why the back door was locked. And the parts that might not reflect well on her and Caleb, merely saying she had to wait a long time until the animals left.

Elizabeth's eyes were big. "Did they ever *kumme* back?"

"*Neh.* Not yet anyway. Caleb put citrus rinds around the *haus.* Skunks don't like the smell of citrus."

"What hypocrites," Irene joked, and everyone laughed again.

And that was how they passed the evening—with laughter, pleasant conversation and good food. They also squeezed in a game of horseshoes between supper and dessert. Rose was on Caleb's team, and although they didn't win, she found she preferred being on his side instead of competing against him, the way she'd done when they'd raced blindfolded.

"You and Caleb ought to pair up for the canoe race in August," Jaala suggested as she helped Rose serve pie afterward. Sadie and Irene quickly echoed the idea.

"*Neh*, absolutely not. It wouldn't be right," Abram interjected, nearly causing Rose to upset the tray of dessert. *Why would he forbid us to pair up?*

His wife asked him the same question. "What's wrong with them being a team?"

"With the lake in their front yard, they have an unfair advantage. They can practice paddling together all the time," he said.

"*Ach!* When do they have time? The work here at the camp keeps them running ragged and on *Suundaag*, the one day when they actually could spend a little leisure time on the lake, you show up to go fishing," Jaala lectured Abram sternly. But Rose noticed a twinkle in his eye; he'd been teasing. She giggled and glanced at Caleb to see his reaction, but he seemed too preoccupied with his pie to look up.

"I promise I won't *kumme* here to fish next week, so you two can practice paddling to your hearts' content," Abram said with a wink at Rose.

Relieved the deacon didn't appear fazed by the idea of Rose and Caleb canoeing together, Rose said, "That's okay. You're *wilkom* anytime. You *all* are." She meant it, too. The *leit* in Serenity Ridge were so warm she already felt as if they were close friends.

In the week that followed, the first blueberries began to ripen, so Rose made haste to pick as many raspberries as she could before she started harvesting the blueberries, too. Because her aunt and uncle didn't have enough land or the right soil for growing wild, or lowbush, blueberries—the kind Maine was famous for—they grew cultivated, or highbush, blueberries. As with the raspberries, Rose would have to pick the blueberries by hand instead of using a rake.

While she hardly had a free moment, she was glad things had returned to normal between Caleb and her, and she couldn't wait to go hiking with him the following Sunday. But as it turned out, the day dawned with a severe thunderstorm, and a steady rain persisted into the evening hours.

Nearly another week passed in the blink of an eye, and Rose was astounded on Friday morning when Hope reminded her at breakfast the blueberry festival was only eight days away.

Rose was incredulous—and frantic. "I thought the blueberry festival wasn't until the last weekend in July?"

"*Jah*, it's on July 30 and 31 this year. That's next Saturday and Sunday."

"What's the blueberry festival?" Caleb asked. He must have forgotten to put his hat on again because his face was nearly as bronzed as his arms, which in turn made his eyes appear nearly as blue as…as *blueberries*. Rose glanced away.

Charity explained the festival was an *Englisch* celebration to kick off the blueberry season. A lot of Maine communities hosted a blueberry festival later in the summer, but Serenity Ridge held theirs early to avoid the competition. Every year women in the district pitched in to rent a tent on the festival grounds so they could sell their goods to locals and tourists. "It's not just baked goods, either. Some women sell blueberry candles or dishcloths with blueberries embroidered onto them. This year Jaala is selling quilts. As long as they're blue or have berries on them, they're fair game."

"You'll sell pies and jam, won't you, Rose?" Caleb asked.

"Jah." Rose explained Jaala and Abram would pick up the items on Saturday morning and sell them for her, since she would be checking guests out and helping the girls prepare the cabins for the next group. "I'll be so busy this week I won't know if I'm coming or going."

"I can help pick berries," Caleb volunteered.

"*Denki*, but I'll manage." Rose hadn't meant to complain; she was only thinking aloud.

"Is there anything I can do to make the week more pleasant for you?"

Warmed by his offer, Rose responded, "*Jah*, you can start it off by canoeing with me on the *Sabbat*."

"That would be a pleasure for me, too," Caleb replied, and Rose thought she heard Eleanor snicker. *Go ahead and tell the deacon you think we're flirting. He won't care!*

But on Sunday, a pair of families who were vacationing together took the canoes and rowboats out on the lake and didn't return until evening. And since Hope and Charity were both feeling under the weather, they came straight home after church. The four of them hung out on the porch, chatting and working on a jigsaw puzzle, which was engaging in its own way, yet not quite the kind of afternoon Rose had hoped to share with Caleb.

The following week Rose spent so much time picking raspberries and blueberries and making jam she gave up trying to remove the little prickles from her wrists or scrub the purple stains from her fingers. One morning she told the twins she'd even had a dream about making jam that was so real she could smell the sweetness in her sleep—only to wake and discover it was her own hands, tucked beneath her cheek, that she'd smelled. But her efforts paid off and by Saturday morning, she had two crates packed with blueberry and mixed-berry jam.

She'd risen at three thirty to make an extra dozen pies for the festival, as well as those for Helen and the produce stand. Jaala and Abram were supposed to arrive at eight, but they still hadn't shown by the time everyone finished breakfast. Checking out guests and cleaning the cabins was always a race against time and Rose didn't have a moment to spare, so Caleb offered to jog to the phone shanty about half a mile down the road to check for a voice mail message.

Some twenty minutes later he reported, "Abram said unfortunately they're both sick. Jaala sends her apologies, but they won't be able to take the pies and jam to the fair."

"Oh, *neh*!" Rose wailed. "Of all the days for this to happen, it had to be changeover day!"

Caleb offered to deliver the goods to the fair himself, but Rose reminded him there was a picture window that needed patching in cabin five and a problem with the bathroom sink in cabin seven. Besides, she doubted he'd want to stick around the festival—he'd be the only man among the half-dozen Amish women selling their wares. And she didn't feel right imposing on one of them to share their display space. "I'll put the pies out on the stand with the others. At least some of them will sell. And the jam will, too, over time..."

"I'll go," Charity volunteered. "You'll be short one person cleaning the cabins and making supper, so it will be tough, but we've managed it before."

Though Rose was skeptical, Caleb convinced her, saying, "I need to run to the hardware store to get screening for the window anyway. So I'll drop Charity off and I can help her cart everything to the tent, too." Hope agreed it was a good idea.

Eleanor was the only one who voiced an objection. "If Hope and I are going to have to work twice as hard, will we get paid twice as much?" she asked, a sly glint in her eyes.

With an equally impish smirk, Rose retorted, "Considering you usually work *half* as hard as you're expected to, you're already getting paid twice as much as you should."

"Hey! I was only teasing!" To Rose's surprise, tears instantly replaced the glint in Eleanor's eyes.

"I was, too," Rose said quickly, even though that was only half-true. "When you're not chatting, you're a *gut* worker. Otherwise, Nancy wouldn't keep you on here." Eleanor crossed her arms over her chest and looked away without acknowledging Rose had spoken.

Caleb broke the tension by announcing he'd go get a folding table for Charity to use and then hitch the horse. Eleanor skulked off to start cleaning, and Hope and

Rose carried pies to the buggy while Charity wheeled the wagon full of jam behind them. As she was handing a crate off to Caleb in the back of the buggy, Charity let go before Caleb had it firmly gripped in his hands, so that his end tipped downward. He managed to right it, but the glass jars clinked hard against each other inside the wooden box.

"Careful!" Rose barked. Maybe she should try to sell these at the stand after all.

Caleb was surprised at how harsh Rose sounded, especially considering he and Charity were doing their best to support her. Her comment to Eleanor hadn't been very kind, either. But he knew how hard she'd labored to make the extra jam and pies this past week and how important earning extra money was to her, so he mumbled an apology before he and Charity took off for the festival.

Within an hour, he was back. As he entered cabin five to patch the screen, he noticed the hinges on the door, as well as on the side window, were rusty. There wasn't enough time to remove and replace them, so he sprayed them with oil and scrubbed them as clean as he could for now. As he worked, the rust brought to mind the verses in Matthew warning against storing treasures where rust or moths could ruin them, and Caleb silently said a prayer for his brother.

Ryan seemed to be growing more despondent the longer the investigation dragged on without resolution and without him being reinstated to his position at the museum. After two weekends of not being able to use the canoe, Caleb was eager to get back on the lake and explore Paradise Point, and he intended to ask Rose to go with him after worship services on Sunday. Although Caleb highly doubted he'd find anything of significance, he at least wanted to be able to tell his brother he was exhausting every last possibility.

It was nearly four o'clock when Caleb finished his other groundskeeper and maintenance duties, including repairing the sink in cabin seven. On his way to the barn he stopped at the dining hall to tell Rose there had been a big crowd at the festival so he was hopeful her pies and jam would sell out. He found her in the kitchen, bent over the sink. She was peeling potatoes so vigorously the skins were flying everywhere. When he entered the room, she turned toward him, glowering. She had a strip of potato in her hair.

"Please don't tell me something went wrong when you took Charity to the festival. I can't take one more bad thing happening today."

"*Neh*, nothing went wrong. The tent is right near the entrance so it was getting a lot of foot traffic, and unloading the jam was a snap," he assured her. "Why, what went wrong here?"

"What didn't?" Rose scooped the peels out of the sink and plopped them in the compost bin. Then she took out the cutting board and a knife and began quartering the potatoes as she recited a litany of mishaps. First, she hadn't realized she'd run out of egg noodles until she began preparing supper. Hope had had to go to town to buy more. Meanwhile, Eleanor claimed to have a stomachache, so Rose didn't want her handling the food and she sent her up to the main house to check in the late arrivals. There were three more *familye* who still weren't there yet, and one of them was lost and kept calling to ask for directions. "I don't know how

I'm going to serve supper on time if I keep getting interrupted."

"I'm not familiar enough with Serenity Ridge to give directions, but I can run the phone up to Eleanor," he volunteered. "And when Hope comes, I'll take care of the buggy so she can hurry back here to help you."

"That would be *wunderbaar.*" Rose handed him the cell phone. "And if it seems like Eleanor is slacking off, send her back down. She might not be able to serve food, but she can empty the compost and sweep the floors. We're not paying her to sit on the porch."

But Eleanor wasn't on the porch when Caleb got to the house. He knocked loudly and opened the door just as she teetered down the hall. Her eyes were watery and her skin was pallid.

"Are you okay?" Caleb asked.

She shook her head. "I just, um…got sick in the bathroom." Shaking, she sat down beside the desk.

"You should go home," he told her.

"*Neh.* Rose needs my help checking guests in. She's making supper alone because Hope had to go get noodles."

"*Jah*, she told me. Listen, I'll go hitch your horse for you and then I'll *kumme* back and check the guests in myself."

Eleanor leaned her head back against the wall and closed her eyes. "*Denki*, Caleb," she said feebly.

When Caleb returned, Hope had the reservation book open on the desk and she pointed to the names of the guests who still hadn't shown up and the numbers of the cabins they'd be staying in. "When they *kumme*, you put a single line through their names so we know they've arrived. If they pay by check, write 'CH' next to their names. If they pay by cash, make a dollar sign.

Then initial the entry. I'll show you where we store the money once they've paid."

She led Caleb to the bookshelf in the gathering room and showed him where the key was hidden beneath the clock and a lockbox was obscured behind tall volumes of encyclopedias. "There are only two more *familye* arriving, so hopefully they'll *kumme* soon."

After Eleanor departed, Caleb took advantage of the opportunity to peruse the reservation book for information about who had stayed at the cabins in mid- to late May. He instantly understood why the FBI was frustrated with Nancy and Sol's record keeping: all they'd recorded were dates, family names and cabin numbers—they didn't even list how many people stayed in each cabin. The most suspicious entry he saw was the name *Smith*, simply because it was so common it could have been used as an alias. After so much anticipation, Caleb was disappointed. *But not nearly as disappointed as Ryan will be when I call him tonight.*

Fortunately, the two families arrived within minutes of each other, and Hope returned shortly after they did. Caleb rushed to the barn to tell her not to unhitch the buggy, since he needed to pick up Charity anyway. He asked Hope to tell Rose that Eleanor needed to go home, but the last customers had arrived and he'd checked them in. At least that was one less interruption Rose would have to contend with while she was preparing supper.

When Caleb got to the tent, Charity exuberantly informed him all of the pies and over half of the jam had sold. Furthermore, Gloria Eicher was staying until the festival ended at eight, so she offered to sell the remaining jars. "Rose will be so pleased, won't she?" Charity exclaimed.

I hope so, Caleb thought. *Because I need her to be in a* gut *mood when I ask if she'll go exploring at Paradise Point tomorrow.*

When Caleb and Charity strolled in as Rose and Hope were clearing the guests' dessert plates from the table, Rose was in a snit. What nerve for Eleanor and Caleb to take it upon themselves to decide Eleanor was going to leave and Caleb was going to check in guests!

"Guess what, Rose? All your *boie* sold—and more than half of the jam, too!" Charity said as she burst through the door.

"Only half the jam?" *That means half the money I was counting on bringing in.*

"*Jah*, but we left the rest with Gloria Eicher. I'm sure even more will sell this evening. The place was packed when we left."

"Oh, so that's what kept you," Rose said, thinking aloud. "Traffic must have been bad."

"*Neh*, we're a few minutes late because on the way out I treated Charity to cotton candy, since one *gut* turn deserves another," Caleb said. "I never saw *blohbier* cotton candy before."

"That was nice of you, but, as you know, Eleanor isn't here, and Hope and I have had to serve supper and clean up ourselves. So now I'm running behind putting our meal on the table." Rose saw the three others exchange glances, but what did they expect of her? She could only work so fast.

After supper was over and the dishes were done, the girls took off with their friends and Caleb left, too.

Usually Rose was glad to have the kitchen to herself, but tonight she was utterly exhausted. Since she wasn't serving meals or baking pies the following day and she'd likely have jam left over from the festival to sell on Monday, she closed up and returned home.

I hope Eleanor doesn't miss work on Muundaag, *too*, she thought as she entered the gathering room. *That's the day I go to the bank, which always cuts into my time.*

After taking the key from its hiding place, she pulled the lockbox out to make sure Caleb had secured the rental payments. She counted the cash and added it to the amount of money they'd received by check. She came up short by one week's worth of rent, so she re-counted it. Again, she was short. There were three checks, which meant five families should have paid in cash. Yet when she tallied the cash a third time, she was still short one week's worth of rent.

She had checked in five *familye*. Three paid by check, two paid in cash. The three guests Eleanor or Caleb had checked in must also have paid in cash or by check. Rose opened the reservation book and discovered Eleanor's initials and a dollar sign next to the Williams family name, which had a line drawn through it. Neither the Jackman nor the Garcia family names were scratched out or had any marking or initials beside them. Obviously Eleanor or Caleb had forgotten to put the payment for one of the *familye* in the lockbox, just like they'd forgotten to record it in the reservation book. Rose regretted ever sending Eleanor up to the house in the first place.

After securing the money, she tromped down to Caleb's cabin to get to the bottom of the matter. Once again, the door was closed—he must have been talking to his brother again—and it took a moment for him to open it.

"I noticed we're missing one week's worth of rent," she told him. "I wondered if you forgot to deposit a payment into the lockbox?"

Caleb wrinkled his forehead. "*Neh.* I checked in two *familye*—the Garcias and the Jackmans. They both paid in cash, and I put their money in the lockbox, just like Eleanor showed me."

"Are you sure? Because the Jackman and Garcia names aren't crossed out and initialed in the reservation book. Didn't she tell you you needed to do that, too?"

Caleb snapped his fingers. "*Ach!* You're right, I completely forgot that part of the process. But I was very careful to put the cash with the rest of the money."

"Are you positive? You were doing a lot of running around today, so maybe you set the money aside before you went to pick up Charity or—"

Caleb squared his shoulders and crossed his arms. "No matter how many times you ask, my answer is going to be the same. I put both payments in the lockbox," he enunciated loudly. "Did you ever consider you or Eleanor forgot to deposit the cash *you* received?"

Rose didn't understand why Caleb was being so defensive—she was only trying to jog his memory. "I'm certain *I* didn't forget. Obviously Eleanor isn't here, so I can't ask her, but since she initialed the one guest she checked in and you didn't initial either of yours, it seemed more likely *you* forgot to lock up the cash, too. Or something."

Caleb didn't appreciate Rose's tone. He felt she was coming dangerously close to accusing him of stealing.

"What do you mean, *or something*? I certainly didn't *take* the money, if that's what you're implying."

"I'm not *implying* anything," Rose echoed scornfully. "I'm trying to figure out why we're one week short of rent."

"Who knows. Maybe someone stole it. Maybe if you had listened to me and locked the doors to your *haus*, we wouldn't be having this conversation."

Rose rolled her eyes. "That's *lecherich.* The *haus* might not have been locked up, but the money was. And even if someone found the key and the lockbox, why would they steal only one week's worth of rent? Why not take *all* the cash that was in there? That doesn't make any sense."

Caleb shrugged. "Then figure it out on your own. All I know is I checked two *familye* in today and I put two weeks' worth of rent in the lockbox. Which, by the way, you never thanked me for doing."

"*Thanked* you?" Rose's voice was shrill. "I never *asked* you to check them in! And *this* kind of mess is exactly why I didn't!"

Caleb's heart felt like a fist of snow. "You're right, you didn't ask. I volunteered. My mistake. It won't happen again." He stepped inside and shoved the door shut with the heel of his boot. His temper flaring, he stood in the middle of the room snorting like a bull before retreating to the bathroom to splash cold water on his face. He'd been about to call Ryan when Rose appeared, but he was too angry to talk right now, so he reopened the front window, as well as the door. Not even the splashing of the water against the shore could calm him.

I've totally wasted my summer, he thought as he peered out over the lake. *I'll spend another week here so I can search the islands and the trails, and then I'm going back to Wisconsin.*

If I don't find that money, I'll have to repay it from my savings. Then how will I ever afford to lease the café? Rose agonized as she lay in bed. Her body desperately craved sleep, but her mind was wide-awake. *And what right did Caleb have to act so indignant?* She hadn't been *accusing* him of taking the rent money. But considering how careless he'd been about recording what he'd received in the reservation book, couldn't he see why she'd wondered if he'd forgotten to lock up the cash, too? If anything, *he* was the one who was judging *her* unfairly by implying she was unappreciative of his help when she'd always tried to express her gratitude…

Eventually, sleep won out and Rose drifted off, but the next morning she felt annoyed all over again, especially when Caleb hardly spoke a word to her or the twins as they waited on the porch for Abram and Jaala to arrive for worship. After nearly half an hour had passed, Charity suggested maybe they were too ill to come, so the four of them read aloud from the book of James and then sang a few hymns, but the atmosphere was so somber it felt more like a funeral than a worship service. Rose was relieved when Hope volunteered to end with a prayer.

No sooner had she said "amen" than someone rapped at the door—Henry stood there with a pink envelope in his hand. After greeting everyone, he handed the note to Rose. "It's from Eleanor. She's sick and wanted you to know she won't be coming to work tomorrow."

Rose thanked him and asked if he'd like to stay for lunch, hoping his presence would lighten the mood, but

Henry said his parents were sick, too, so he needed to get home. "My *mamm* wanted me to ask if you have any peppermint tea or ginger root she can have."

"*Jah*, I'll get it," Charity said.

"And I'll box up some mac and cheese, and cut you a piece of *boi*," Hope offered. "If your *mamm* and *schweschder* are both ill, they won't be preparing meals today."

Henry followed the twins into the kitchen, leaving Caleb and Rose alone.

"So, Eleanor is actually sick," Caleb said after an awkward pause. "Imagine that."

"What do you mean?" Rose asked.

"You acted as if she wasn't really ill. I suppose you thought *she* was lying, too."

"I never said anyone was lying!" Rose protested. But deep down, she knew he was right—about Eleanor anyway. Rose *had* suspected she *was* feigning illness, maybe to get back at Rose for her wisecrack. She justified her attitude by telling herself, *Caleb would have thought the same thing if he knew Eleanor like I do.* "I'll go make lunch," she said.

"Count me out. I'm not *hungerich*."

Now who's lying? Not that she cared if he joined them; it had been a long time since she'd eaten alone with her cousins and she was looking forward to it. But after they sent Henry off with a container of remedies and food, Hope and Charity told Rose their friends were picnicking on Black Bear Lake. "We'll stop to see if Jaala and Abram need anything on our way there," Hope said.

So, after changing out of her best dress, Rose made a sandwich and carried it to the porch, where she began writing a letter to Nancy. After inquiring about Sol's health, she wrote, *Because of the blueberry festival, we had a chaotic day yesterday, but Charity and Hope came to the rescue...* Rose set down her pen and reflected on all that the girls—and Caleb—had done to help her sell jam and pies at the festival, and she was overwhelmed with shame. Caleb was right; she'd hardly so much as uttered a word of thanks. Instead, she'd snapped at them and bellyached about all the work *she* had to do.

Bellyache—the word reminded her she hadn't read Eleanor's note yet. She retrieved it from the house and opened it to discover a wad of bills folded inside. *"Dear Rose..."* She read as she stood near the porch railing. The word *dear* made Rose feel even guiltier about her attitude toward the young woman. *"I have a high fever and won't be able to come to work until it's gone. I had to run to the bathroom so quickly yesterday I didn't have time to lock up the rent from the Williams family. I tucked the money into my sleeve and forgot about it until I changed last night. Hope you weren't looking for it!—Eleanor."*

Rose didn't know whether to laugh or cry. But she did know she had to apologize. She locked the money in the box and ran to Caleb's cabin. Halfway there, she spotted him on the beach, donning a life vest.

"Caleb, wait!" she called, but he continued preparing to go out on the water. She dashed toward him. "Eleanor had the money—it was in her note. She'd collected it but, because she was sick, she forgot to put it in the lockbox."

"Is that right?" he said dryly, not looking up as he

pushed the canoe across the sand. Rose tugged on the side so he couldn't propel it into the water.

"Caleb, please, *absatz*. This is important." He scowled at her, but at least he made eye contact. "I'm sorry I thought you misplaced the rent."

"You didn't think I misplaced it—you thought I *stole* it."

She gasped. "*Neh*, that's not true. I didn't think you stole it, not for a second. I know you're not a thief. I just thought you were, you know, careless or forgetful or something."

"Am I supposed to be flattered? You don't think I'm a thief, just that I'm incompetent?"

Rose's eyes brimmed. "*Neh*, I don't think you're incompetent. You were doing so much to help me yesterday I figured your head was spinning as much as mine was, that's all." She let go of the canoe and straightened her posture to wipe away the tears that were now streaming down her cheeks. "But I was wrong to think you'd been careless. And wrong to think Eleanor was faking being sick. As you said, I was terribly unappreciative yesterday. My behavior didn't reflect how highly I think of you and how grateful I am for your support. I'm sorry from the bottom of my heart. What can I do to make it up to you?"

Caleb was moved by Rose's words and pained by her tears. How was it possible he could be so angry with her one day and want to take her in his arms the next? He'd never experienced anything like this in a relationship before. Oh, he'd experienced his share of arguments, but he'd never received an apology like Rose's, perhaps because he'd always run away instead of reconciling.

He'd intended to run this time, too, but Rose's contrition changed everything. "You can help me paddle to the islands. I want to go exploring."

"Th-then you'll forgive me?" She sniffed and blotted her eyes with her apron.

"*Neh*, I already forgive you," he said, and it was true. The bitterness he'd felt was gone, just like that. "*Kumme*, before someone from *kurrich* shows up and wants to go fishing with me."

But Rose said she needed to leave a note for Hope and Charity, and she dashed off to the house. She returned a couple minutes later carrying a cooler and a jug. They paddled to the smallest island first, which was exactly as Rose had described it: a lump of land with a few rocks and trees poking out of it. Caleb doubted anyone would hide anything there. It looked as if a good rain could raise the water high enough to submerge it. The second island was only slightly larger, so after a quick stop there, he suggested they take a detour to Relaxation Rock before heading to Paradise Point.

They were almost to shore when the white sky spit a few hot, fat raindrops at them and thunder rolled in the distance. Fortunately, they made it to land before the clouds really let loose. This time, they took extra care to pull the canoe completely out of the water.

"Follow me," Rose called over her shoulder. She led him down a trail to a wooden birding pavilion, which contained a bench barely big enough for two people. Rose set the jug between them and Caleb placed the cooler at his feet. After pouring them each a cup of lemonade, she shifted sideways to face him. Her eyes were clouded and he hoped she wouldn't cry again. "It's really important you know I never thought you'd stolen the rent, Caleb."

"I do know," he acknowledged. Her expression was so concerned Caleb found himself admitting, "I probably overreacted to what you said because, well, because my *bruder* was once wrongly accused of being a thief and it's nearly destroying—it nearly *destroyed* his entire life. His job, his *familye*, his well-being…"

Rose inhaled sharply. "That's *baremlich*!"

"Jah." Caleb realized he'd better stop talking; Rose was so sympathetic and easy to talk to he might just break down and tell her everything.

"No wonder you were upset when I questioned you about the money," she acknowledged. "But I never, ever thought you'd stolen it—"

"Rose, you don't have to keep apol—"

"*Shh*, please let me explain," she said, putting a finger to her lips. Oh, her rosy lips. "I think I've told you about my former fiancé, Baker… Well, the fact is he stole money from my business account. He confessed to it and everything, so it wasn't as if he was wrongly accused. My point in telling you this is to say I know you're absolutely nothing like Baker. I know you're a man of integrity."

Caleb's mind was spinning like a tornado. He was simultaneously delighted and devastated to hear Rose's words. *Would she still think that if she knew I'm* Englisch*? Would the reason I've been pretending to be Amish make a difference?*

"Caleb?" she said, touching his arm lightly. It set his skin afire.

"*Denki.* I appreciate you sharing that with me," he responded.

"Then why are you looking at me like that?"

Because I can't look away from you. A teeny spider dotted the white kerchief Rose was wearing as a head covering. He reached toward her. "There's a little insect by your ear, here," he said. She lowered her eyelids as he wiped it away with his thumb. His fingers were so close to her chin he wanted to cup it in his hand. To draw her near and kiss her. Neither of them moved. The air felt charged, the way it does right before a lightning strike.

But no, he couldn't. It was one thing to pose as an Amish man: that was a necessary deception. But he couldn't cause Rose to break the rules of the *Ordnung* by unwittingly kissing an *Englischer.* Reluctantly, he withdrew his hand and cleared his throat.

"Looks like the rain has let up. How about if we go for a walk?" he said.

Chapter Eight

"Kiss and make up." The expression occurred to Rose several times during the week following her conversation with Caleb at Relaxation Rock. She was so sure he'd been about to kiss her as they sat together in the pavilion, and she was equally sure she'd wanted him to. For a fleeting second anyway. But the more days that went by without any additional signs Caleb was romantically interested in her, the more preposterous the possibility seemed in hindsight. Yes, Rose valued his friendship as much as he seemed to value hers, but they weren't courting, so a kiss wouldn't have been appropriate. Besides, in less than a month, they'd go their separate ways. *I have too much to do to be distracted by a passing moment of attraction. I'm glad* Gott *brought Caleb and me here at the same time, but a suitor doesn't fit into my long-term plans.*

Since Rose projected she was still several hundred dollars short of securing the lease on the café, she intended to double up on her baking and jam-making efforts. But Eleanor's absence meant Rose had to leave the fields earlier than usual to prepare supper, and cleanup took her and the twins longer, too. When Eleanor returned, Rose needed to let her know how much she'd missed her help. Unfortunately, her young coworker's illness lasted through the week and by Friday, Rose was so drained she forgot all about collecting the money jar and unsold produce from the roadside stand until after supper.

As she approached the little building, she spied a pair of crows pecking at the ground in front of it. At first Rose guessed a customer must have spilled a pint of berries, but then she saw it was piecrust the birds were eating. *Ach! I wonder if the customer paid for that pie before dropping it.* But when Rose got closer, she noticed a thick purple splat across the "Rose's Pies" sign and she realized someone had smashed the pie against it on purpose. She couldn't imagine anyone in their district wasting food like that.

It was probably an Englischer, she grumbled to herself. It must have been one of the tourists she'd seen slowing their cars to photograph her in the fields lately—the local *Englischers* were too respectful to snap pictures or destroy property like this. Rose sighed. Sometimes it felt like for each step she took forward, she took two steps backward and three steps sideways, getting further and further from her goal, and it made her wonder if *Gott* really wanted her to have a business of her own after all.

She loaded the wagon with unsold items and carefully balanced the sign atop them. Back at the barn she scrubbed and scrubbed until the stubborn blueberry stain faded, and then she trekked to the road again to put the sign back in its place. There was still a faint blotch of blue clouding Rose's name and she hoped Caleb wouldn't notice it. Knowing what he was like, if she told him about the vandalism—which was actually more like graffiti, really—he'd probably suggest they needed to bolt their windows now, in addition to their doors.

When she got back to the house, Rose tallied the amount of produce and jam that hadn't been sold, and then counted the money deposited in the mayonnaise jar. She was heartened to find she had a dollar more than she would have expected, which meant someone had actually paid for the smashed pie. It was a trifling amount, but Rose received the additional profit almost as if it were the Lord encouraging her to keep going. She returned to the dining hall and prepared the ingredients for Saturday's pies with a smile on her face and a song of thanks on her lips.

She was even more joyful on Saturday morning when Eleanor showed up in the dining hall. "I'm *hallich* you're back," Rose said as she embraced her tall, thin coworker. "I really struggled without you here."

Eleanor pulled away to meet Rose's eyes. "*Jah*, but it was probably a lot quieter without me around, wasn't it?"

Rose bit her lip, but then Eleanor giggled and Rose knew she didn't have to answer; everything was all right between them again. "Since you're here, I'm going to run to the produce stand, okay? Helen needs to pick up her pies early today."

With her hair sticking out and a coffee stain on the front of her shirt, Helen looked as frazzled as Rose had felt all week. "I had a rowdy group at the inn last night," she explained. "Looks like you might have had trouble here, too. What happened to your sign?"

When Rose told her, Helen responded much the same

as Caleb would have reacted—by suggesting Rose call the police. Rose shook her head. "It was probably just a group of bored kids playing a prank. And they paid for the pie—there wasn't any money missing from the jar."

"I wouldn't care whether they paid for the pie or not. It wasn't right of them to ruin your sign!" Helen exclaimed. "You're a lot more forgiving than I am."

Helen's comment returned to Rose later that afternoon when she saw Baker's penmanship on an envelope she pulled from the mailbox. She was racked with guilt. *I'm so unforgiving I don't even want to read anything he has to say*, she thought, and tossed the letter on the hall table.

It wasn't until she was headed upstairs for bed that she resigned herself to reading it. *"Dear Rose,"* it began, and Rose was grateful he hadn't taken the liberty of using his nickname for her again.

> *Your mother told me you've been busy baking pies to sell—she said that's probably why I haven't heard back from you myself. I hope it's not because you're still angry at me. I know what I did was wrong, but I really* have *changed, Rose.*
>
> *I've been learning a lot from working at the hardware store. It's got me thinking about opening a harness shop since I have so many connections with horse and stable owners. Maybe you and I could even co-lease that little building on Fourth and Main—you know, where the bookstore used to be. They sold food there, too, so there's got to be an oven for you to use, and I could set up shop in the rest of the space. What do you think?*

Won't be long until you're back home. Meanwhile, I wanted you to know how much I've missed you.
Yours,
Baker.

Rose closed her eyes and shook her head. If it wasn't that Caleb would come running to see what was wrong, she might have screamed her lungs out. Instead, she smacked her mattress with her fist. *He just doesn't get it! I don't want to be his business partner and I don't want to partner with him in a courtship, either! Why won't he leave me alone? Our courtship is over! It's in the past.*

And that's when it really sank in: she *had* forgiven Baker for stealing from her; she was no longer angry about that. She'd released him. But *he* hadn't released *her*—and *that* was what was angering her now. For her own sake, as well as for his, she couldn't put it off any longer; she was going to have to set him straight.

Rose dropped to her knees. *Oh, Lord,* she prayed. *Please give me the words to express what I need to say, and please give Baker the ears to really hear me. I don't want to hurt him,* Gott...

After meditating a long time, Rose stood and pulled a sheet of paper from the drawer. *"Dear Baker,"* she began. *"Thank you for your letters and for the payments. I do believe you are changing and growing. So am I, by God's grace. While I honestly don't hold any ill will toward you, neither do I have any interest in a courtship or a professional relationship with you in the future. But you will always be my brother in Christ, and because of that I'll pray for God's best for you. (For me, too!) Take care, Rose."*

After folding the letter and sliding it into an envelope, Rose changed into her nightgown and then stretched out on her bed. She expected she'd feel at peace now that she'd finally written to Baker. Instead, she felt agitated by her own words. Was staying single and owning a restaurant really *Gott*'s best for her? And if it was, why couldn't she stop imagining what it would be like to have Caleb as her suitor?

Caleb had been calling his brother all evening, but Ryan wasn't answering. It was eleven thirty in Maine, which meant it was ten thirty in Chicago. *Why isn't he picking up? He never misses our weekly calls.* It was too hot to keep the windows and doors closed the way he usually did when he called Ryan, so Caleb reopened them. A rush of cool air lifted Caleb's hair from his forehead. That was better, he thought as he sank into the armchair.

His thoughts turned to Rose, as they tended to do lately. Ever since she had apologized to him and he'd confided in her about his brother, Caleb had been tormented by his feelings for Rose. He'd never been in a relationship with a woman that involved the kind of emotional vulnerability he'd shared with her, and because of this closeness, a part of him regretted not kissing her when he'd had the chance.

But not kissing her had been the honorable thing to do. To *not* do. A hundred times a day Caleb reminded himself that no matter how drawn he was to Rose, he couldn't deceive her by acting the way a boyfriend would act. Reminded himself that even if she were drawn to him, a courtship with her would be impossible. He might be able to hide it awhile longer, but eventually she'd find out he was *Englisch* and she'd be devastated. Caleb couldn't hurt her like that, especially not after how Baker betrayed her trust. Then it occurred to Caleb he was betraying Rose's trust himself—the difference was that she didn't know about it.

And he'd do whatever he could to ensure she never found out, but that didn't mean keeping his distance from her again. *Today is August 6, which means I have a month left to spend with Rose and I'm going to make the most of it!* Unfortunately, he also only had a month left to search for the coins, which had kept him so busy he wasn't able to chat with Rose nearly as often as he wanted. Either he was busy searching the woods or making his way along the rocks on the shoreline near the cabins, or she was consumed by picking berries and rolling piecrusts.

"But tomorrow's *Suundaag*," he said aloud as he tapped the icon next to Ryan's name on his cell phone. "Which means I can go canoeing with her..."

When his brother's voice mail came on, Caleb disconnected, waited a few minutes and tried again, to no avail. *Where could he be?* Caleb envisioned Ryan being taken into custody, and he immediately began to pray for peace for himself and for his brother, wherever he was and whatever was happening to him. Not five minutes later, Caleb received a text saying, Sorry, can't talk now. Everything's OK. Can u call me tomorrow after church?

Sure. 2 EST, he texted back, perplexed but relieved Ryan was okay. Caleb pulled the Bible off the top of the dresser. Reading it had become his nightly practice, and it was such a source of wisdom and comfort he was glad he hadn't brought any other books with him to Serenity Ridge.

It was past midnight when he turned off the lamp, but Caleb couldn't turn off his thoughts; once again, they were mostly of Rose. *Ach! I won't be able to go canoeing with her tomorrow until after I call Ryan!* The delay would set him back only a half hour or so, but even thirty minutes felt like a big loss when he considered how quickly summer was drawing to a close. *At least I'll get to ride home alone with her*, he comforted himself before rolling over and finally dozing off to sleep.

On the way to church the following morning, Hope piped up from the back of the buggy, "We figure we ought to tell you this now, Rose and Caleb, before you hear it from someone else at *kurrich*. Last night at the carnival, a group of us bumped into Oliver Graham and his friends again."

Although most Amish considered the carnival too worldly to attend, Caleb was aware it was a popular gathering place for Amish teens during their *rumspringa*. "Did he bother you?" he asked.

"Well, he didn't *do* anything. But his *onkel* is a detective and Oliver overheard him talking on the phone last weekend at their *familye* reunion. Oliver said the law enforcement agencies are closing in on the thief, and when they find him, *Mamm* and *Daed* will be arrested for aiding and abetting a criminal."

"That's *lecherich*!" Rose and Caleb exclaimed in unison.

Charity added, "He said we have limited time to decide whether we're more afraid of what the criminal will do if we turn him in or what a prosecutor will do if we conceal evidence."

"Conceal evidence?" Rose scoffed. "What evidence?"

"According to Oliver, the stolen coins are hidden somewhere on our property and we know where they are but we're using our religion as an excuse not to get involved."

Caleb was incensed but Rose actually chuckled. "That's *narrish*!"

"*Jah*, but not as *narrish* as Oliver's friend, Clint Dale, telling everyone when he was hunting near our property last week he saw *Mamm* carrying a shovel through the woods," Charity ranted. "He said she was probably moving the coins to a new hiding place so the thief could pick them up without being intercepted at our *haus* by the police."

"I told him *Mamm* couldn't possibly have done that because *Mamm* and *Daed* haven't even been home for over a month." Hope sounded smug about proving Clint wrong, but Caleb inwardly moaned, realizing she'd essentially announced the women were staying alone in the house.

Charity harrumphed. "You'd have thought that would have shut them—I mean stopped them from saying anything else. But Oliver suggested *Mamm* and *Daed* probably fled to Canada because they want to avoid the court system, just like the Amish avoid paying taxes."

"But we *do* pay taxes!" Rose said, referring to the fact they essentially paid the same taxes as the *Englisch* except for Medicare, Social Security and self- and unemployment taxes, since the Amish didn't collect those benefits. "That goes to show Oliver doesn't have any idea what he's talking about."

Caleb broke in, "Regardless, I think it's time I have a talk with Oliver's *onkel*."

"The detective? Why? Because of some ludicrous stories a couple *buwe* concocted to antagonize the *meed*?" Rose's voice was high-pitched and wary. "You know that isn't our way."

"Not usually, *neh*, but this isn't a *familye* matter or an issue between members of our *kurrich* that can be resolved with help from the bishop or deacon," Caleb reasoned. "This is about our safety. If there's a chance a criminal might return to the camp for stolen goods, we should be kept informed. Also, it's possible law enforcement could send a police officer to keep watch on the camp for our protection."

"*Gott* is protecting us!" Rose sputtered. "We don't need any more police presence at the camp. *Ant* Nancy said it was very disruptive the first time. We heard rumors similar to this last month and nothing came of them."

Caleb figured it was better not to argue on the way to church; better not to *argue* at all, especially since he didn't want to do anything to jeopardize spending an afternoon alone with Rose. He didn't reply, and the girls' conversation turned to the topic of the fish fry and canoe race coming up at the end of the month.

"How many *leit* do you think will *kumme* from Unity?" Hope asked Charity.

Charity's reply was barely audible, but Caleb thought she said, "What you really want to know is whether Gideon's cousin from Unity is coming, isn't it?" Her question was followed by giggling and whispering that kept up until they arrived at church.

The deacon's sermons usually captivated Caleb's attention—he particularly appreciated hearing portions of the Bible read in German—but today he was engrossed in thinking about what Oliver had told Charity and Hope. Caleb couldn't fathom any detective worth his salt discussing an ongoing investigation, but he *could* imagine Oliver being sneaky enough to eavesdrop on his uncle.

Yet how much of what Oliver said was an accurate representation of what he had possibly overheard and how much was fabricated? From other comments the teen had made to the twins, it was clear to Caleb he resented the Amish. But did that necessarily invalidate his remarks about law enforcement closing in on the thief? Or about the thief returning to the camp? Most of Oliver's claims were outlandish, but a few had an element of plausibility. It was kind of like what he said about the Amish not paying taxes—he was partly wrong, yet partly right. Caleb stewed. Was he partly right about the situation with the coin thief, too?

As the twins expected, other parents had been told about the rumors, and while Caleb was eating lunch with the men after the worship service, Miriam Lapp's father said, "We heard a young *bu* has been taunting Charity and Hope about their *eldre*, saying they're linked to that matter the FBI was investigating this spring."

"*Jah*, my *suh* told me the same thing last night," Gideon Eicher's father commented. "Such a shame to torment the twins like that, especially when their *daed* is so sick."

Caleb was glad the subject was out in the open. Now he could solicit the men's advice about whether or not he ought to talk to Oliver's uncle. "What do you think I should do about it?" he asked.

"Rcmind them to avoid the *bu*. To walk in the other direction if they see him coming. It takes two to argue."

Caleb hadn't meant what should he do about the girls interacting with Oliver—he meant what should he do if what Oliver said was true.

Abram seemed to have caught the gist of Caleb's question. "Are you concerned there might actually be a criminal returning to the camp?"

Caleb tried to sound nonchalant. "It has crossed my mind, *jah*."

"Have you seen anyone suspicious on the property, or has anything out of the ordinary happened?"

Caleb racked his memory. Twigs snapping in the woods. A canoe floating away. An open drawer… Each of these occurrences could have a logical explanation, and he'd seem foolish if he told the other men about them. "*Neh*, not really," he admitted.

"Then I don't think you ought to do anything at this time except pray. Let's do that now." Caleb and the deacon bowed their heads, as did the other men at the table. "Lord, we ask Your protection for Charity, Hope, Rose and Caleb. Protect them from fear, as well as from danger. Give them strength to respond with grace to those who might wish to trouble them. We ask for healing for Sol, too. *Denki*, Lord for being our very present help in trouble. Amen."

Abram clapped Caleb's shoulder, adding, "I'm glad you're staying at the camp—I know Sol feels better you're there, too. And I think it's wise to be vigilant. We'll stop by from time to time to check in, but if there's anything you need before then, let us know."

Caleb appreciated the support and vote of confidence. He was also comforted because instead of suggesting Caleb lacked faith or was overreacting, Abram recommended remaining vigilant. But Caleb realized it was Abram's prayer, above all, that had given him a sense of real peace.

When he returned home and called his brother, Caleb heard a woman giggling in the background, along with Liam's laughter. *Who could* that *be?* "It sounds like you have company."

"No, not company. Sheryl's here. We just got back from church and we're getting ready to eat lunch. We, uh, camped out together last night—all three of us, in a tent in the backyard. That's why I didn't pick up. I forgot all about our scheduled call and left my phone in the house. I happened to notice it vibrating when I went inside to use the bathroom."

Caleb was happy Ryan and Sheryl seemed to have found some common ground so Liam wouldn't have to listen to their incessant arguing. He told Ryan the latest news and asked if his brother had heard similar rumors.

"No, no one has updated me about anything recently, so as far as I know, the investigation is still open. Waiting is agony. Thank the Lord I have Liam and Sheryl to distract me," Ryan said, which surprised Caleb. He didn't think going through a divorce was considered a welcome distraction. His brother hedged, "You don't suppose it's possible that..."

"That what?"

"That Nancy and Sol really do know more than they've been letting on?"

"No!" Caleb barked. There were many questionable possibilities in his mind, but Nancy and Sol's truthfulness was not one of them. He lowered his voice to repeat, "No. Absolutely not. The Amish might not actively seek out the police for matters they can resolve on their own, but they're law-abiding citizens. More important, they obey God's law, which means if they were questioned, they wouldn't lie—especially not to protect a criminal. I'm as sure about that as I am about...about the fact *you're* not the thief!"

"Okay, okay, I hear you. I'm sorry. I didn't mean to question their integrity, I only wanted to rule that possibility out," Ryan apologized.

"That's the problem. How can you and I rule anything out—or in? What do we really have to go on? A cryptic, anonymous note? Something a teenage kid said? Conjecture?" Caleb usually tried to put a positive spin on the situation in order to buoy his brother's hope, but right now he was having difficulty keeping his own perspective afloat. Summer was wrapping up and Caleb felt he was no closer to discovering anything worthwhile than when he'd first arrived.

"Maybe you *should* go have a chat with that detective. Get a sense of what's what. Find out if you're in any jeopardy. It's possible the police want to surveil the camp but out of respect for the Amish, they're not."

"I can't," Caleb said, remembering how aghast Rose had been at the idea. "It's not the Amish way and I'd draw attention to myself. I can't blow my cover now." *I can't* ever *blow my cover.*

"Hey, listen, as much as I'd love for you to find the coins, I don't want you to take any unnecessary chances." Ryan's voice cracked. "I'd rather go to prison than have anything happen to you, Caleb."

Startled by the intensity of his brother's sentiment, Caleb made light of his concerns, which had been his concerns, too, until the deacon prayed for him. "What could possibly happen? For all we know, the note you got was a ploy to distract everyone while the thief was taking off for Mexico. And while he was on his road trip, he probably spent the coins in every vending machine between Chicago and Cancún!" When Ryan didn't laugh, Caleb grew serious again. "Even if what Oliver Graham told the girls about the thief coming back is true, there's nothing to suggest he plans to harm anyone. The heist was a white-collar crime. The thief is greedy, not violent."

"The prospect of losing a million dollars' worth of stolen property can turn a greedy person into a violent one pretty quickly," Ryan countered.

"If that's the case, I'm sure the police are on top of it. The FBI is on top of it. It's likely they're already surveilling the camp. Like you said, they're just not telling us about it because we're Amish and they know it violates our principles."

Ryan chuckled. "*We're* Amish?"

"What?"

"You said *we're* Amish and it violates *our* principles," Ryan echoed. "You do know you're still… What do the Amish call us? *Englisch*, right?"

Sometimes, I wish I weren't, Caleb thought. *I wish I could stay here forever because, even in the midst of all this chaos, I feel more tranquil and at home now than I have since...since I lived with the Amish in Pennsylvania.* "Yeah, the Amish would consider us *Englischers*."

"Speaking of *Englisch*—or actually, of German—the other day I received the mail you had forwarded from your home. You got a big envelope from the university."

"That's probably my teaching contract for the year. I've got to sign it before the semester begins. Could you put it in a plain envelope and send it to me here? I don't want anyone to see the university's return address."

"Then you're definitely staying in Maine longer? You really don't have to—especially if you think you're at risk."

"I know that. But I want to." *Not just because of the hunt for the coins, either.*

"A couple weeks ago you were concerned about the dangers of staying there and now you're insisting you won't leave. What changed?"

"God is sovereign, so what do I have to fear?" Caleb said, paraphrasing Rose. "But promise you'll do one thing."

"Whatever you need."

"Pray for me—for all of us here."

"I already have been praying, but I'll keep it up."

"Denki," Caleb said. Then, realizing he'd spoken in Amish, he clarified, "That means *thank you* in *Deitsch*."

"Bitte schön," Ryan replied.

"That's *you're welcome* in German, not in *Deitsch*, but it's not bad for an *Englischer*," Caleb told him, and their call ended with both of them laughing.

For once, instead of Hope and Charity running off to Miriam Lapp's house after church, Miriam had accompanied the twins back to the camp. Rose was relieved; considering the conversation they'd had with Oliver Graham, she preferred that Hope and Charity not hang out where they might bump into him. Not because she gave what Oliver had said any weight, but because it had resulted in Charity and Hope being upset—and it had almost resulted in an argument between Rose and Caleb, too.

The girls were in the kitchen gathering snacks, including the blueberry muffins left over from last night's supper, to take with them canoeing. Rose managed to sneak one for herself and she ambled out onto the porch with it, thinking about Caleb. He had seemed a lot more relaxed on the way home than on the way to *kurrich.* She wondered what he was up to right now.

She'd barely sat down when he sauntered up the path and settled into the other glider. "Hi, Ro—oh, muffins! Have you got any more of those?"

"You can have this one." She handed him her muffin. "I don't know why I took it—I'm not the least bit *hungerich.*"

"Do you have to be *hungerich* to eat a *blohbier* muffin?" Caleb's grin outshone his eyes. Or maybe it was that his eyes illuminated his grin.

"I'll get you a glass of *millich.*" As she was inside pouring it, Rose heard the cell phone ring, but she didn't take business calls on the Sabbath. When she returned to the porch, the muffin was gone and Caleb was brushing crumbs off his lap. Rose extended the glass to him before taking her seat again.

He accepted the milk, then immediately set it aside and leaned forward, resting his forearms against his knees. "Listen, Rose, there's something I need to speak to you about, and I'd like you to hear me out before you say *neh.*"

Her heartbeat rattled. For the briefest moment she wondered if he was going to ask to court her. How would she answer? "Go on," she replied.

"I'm sorry I suggested we should go to the police. After talking to Abram and praying about it, I realized I was letting my concern—my *fear* that something might happen to you or to the twins—get the best of me. So, I want you to know I have no intention of contacting Oliver Graham's *onkel*."

Rose's ears and cheeks stung; how silly she'd been to imagine he'd ask to be her suitor. Yet how sweet it was to hear him express concern for her and the girls. "*Denki*. I appreciate that." She smiled, though Caleb's forehead was riddled with lines.

"But I still think it's important to exercise caution. So, I'd like to suggest you and the *meed* consider not going off canoeing or hiking on your own. I think there should always be at least two people together."

"Is this your indirect way of asking me to go hiking with you?" Rose quipped. There it was—she *knew* she could spark a smile across Caleb's lips again.

"I *do* hope you'll *kumme* hiking with me this afternoon, *jah*, but I also hope you'll agree not to go into the woods or canoeing alone."

"Okay, sure," she said, nodding. Once again she could hear the cell phone in the background; she should have silenced the volume when she was inside getting milk. "I'll tell Charity and Hope not to wander off alone, either—although the two of them are usually inseparable anyway."

"Wow." Caleb leaned back in his chair. "I didn't think you'd agree so easily."

"Oh, I'm still not concerned we're in any danger, and I don't want us to lose our wits again, but this seems to mean a lot to you, so pairing up instead of going out alone is a small concession for me to make," she explained.

"*Denki*. It *does* mean a lot to me." Caleb's eyes gleamed as he added, "It means so much that if you said *neh* I was prepared to cash in the favor you owe me! I'm glad I didn't have to."

Rose tittered. "Well, don't wait too long—that favor expires when we head our separate ways in four weeks." At the thought of summer ending, Rose was gripped with apprehension. Not merely because she was still over five hundred dollars short of her financial goal, but also because she was going to miss this place. These people. Hope and Charity and Caleb. *Especially Caleb.*

"I actually already have something in mind—" Caleb said, but he was interrupted by Hope charging through the screen door in tears, Charity on her heels and Miriam wringing her hands behind both of them.

"That was *Mamm* on the phone," Hope sobbed. "*Daed*'s health has taken a turn for the worse. She wants us to *kumme* join her in Ohio as soon as we can."

Chapter Nine

Rose leaped to her feet and enveloped both of the twins in her arms. She wanted to tell them everything was going to be all right, their father was going to be fine—or maybe she wanted someone to say that to *her*—but she knew she couldn't give them false hope, so she just held on to them. After a few moments, the girls pulled away and Hope wiped her eyes. "I'll help you pack, but let's pray first, okay?" Rose asked.

She extended a hand, palm up, to Hope on one side and to Caleb on the other. Caleb reached for Charity's hand, and she reached for Miriam's, and Miriam completed the circle by taking Hope's opposite hand. They bowed their heads and shut their eyes. Too distraught to pray aloud herself, Rose squeezed Caleb's fingers and whispered, "Could you?"

"Our Lord *Gott*, we *kumme* to you with troubled hearts," Caleb began somberly. Hope caught her breath, and Rose feared the young woman would break into tears again as Caleb continued, "We're concerned about Sol's health, yet we know You're the great physician, the One who can heal all our illnesses and forgive all our sins. We don't know what Your sovereign will is for Sol's life, but our prayer is that You'd make him well again."

As Caleb asked *Gott* to give Charity and Hope a safe and trouble-free trip, Rose cherished the feeling of his warm hand engulfing hers. She had the same sense of being able to trust him to accompany her on this dark journey that she'd had when he led her down the path from Paradise Point on the Fourth of July.

After he finished praying, Miriam said, "*Kumme*, Hope and Charity. I'll help you with your suitcases."

The girls were following her into the house when Charity said, "We have to tell Ivy and Arleta we won't be able to mind the *kinner* this week. They'll need to know soon so they can find someone else to help."

"I'll go tell them," Caleb offered. "I can arrange for a van driver to pick you up in the morning, too."

"What about you?" Hope asked Rose. "How will you manage by yourself?"

"I'm not by myself. I have Eleanor and Caleb," Rose assured her, even though she had the same misgivings about how she'd keep up with everything at the camp.

"I'd love to help you serve breakfast and clean up in the mornings," Miriam volunteered. "It will give me a break from taking care of my *breider*."

"Oh, but I was going to ask if you'd watch Ivy's *kinner* in my place," Charity suggested.

"No way! I'd rather watch my *breider*!" Miriam's expression of dismay momentarily caused the twins to giggle. "I'll ask my *mamm* to help find a *maedel* to care for Ivy's *kinner*."

"Don't fret about those details now. We'll work

things out later so no one is left short staffed," Rose told them.

But as she lay in bed that evening, she struggled to create a plan for keeping up with the responsibilities of running the camp and harvesting the produce, while also making pies and jam for her own profit. Amity Speicher, a newlywed and the district's schoolteacher, might be available to cover one of the girls' mother's-helper jobs—until school began again anyway. Maybe Mildred Schwartz could give a hand to the other mother? As for making pies, Rose thought, *Helen said she'd be flexible if something came up and I couldn't bake...* But she quickly rejected the idea of canceling Helen's standing pie order. It was a reliable source of extra income, and Rose didn't want to let the *Englischer* down. She'd just have to rise even earlier or go to bed even later than she'd already been doing.

Rose pulled the sheet to her chin and rolled over. But instead of slumbering, she watched the shadows of pine branches dancing on the wall until she couldn't keep her eyes open any longer. Nearby, a loon wailed plaintively. *I know exactly how you feel*, she thought, and drifted off to sleep.

Not long after Caleb had taken Miriam home and informed Ivy and Arleta that Hope and Charity were going to Ohio to be with their parents, a series of storms bowled across the lake, and even now gusts of wind clapped choppy waves against the rocks outside his window. But that wasn't what was keeping him awake; Caleb was anguished over Sol's health and bothered by the idea of Rose staying in the house completely alone.

Since he couldn't sleep anyway, he got out of bed

and took the Bible off the dresser top to continue reading where he'd left off. As he flipped the leather cover open, he came across the photo of Liam. Caleb recalled how he'd told his nephew he'd come back to Chicago and go camping with him as soon as possible. That felt like a lifetime ago and he wondered how many teeth Liam had lost since then. He tucked the photo away and exchanged the Bible for a sheet of paper and a pen.

"Sol," he wrote. *"I'm sorry you've been so ill. I will continue praying for you daily."*

> *Things are going well here at the camp. The beans, broccoli and cucumbers are flourishing. The potatoes were infested with aphids earlier in the season, but the mums and zinnias have attracted enough ladybugs to remedy that situation.*
>
> *Please greet Nancy for me and let her know Rose, Charity and Hope have kept everyone happy and well-fed. One guest even sent a thank-you note saying he gained seven pounds while his family was here—but it was worth it. (I could say the same thing myself!)*
>
> *I reeled in a couple four-pound trout a few weeks ago, but the twins told me you've caught fish twice that size. You'll have to show me what I'm doing wrong when you return at the end of August.*

Caleb reread the letter before signing it, and then he uttered another prayer for Sol's health and went back to bed. He woke extra early to collect eggs and milk the cow so Hope and Charity wouldn't have to—he wanted them to get as much sleep as they could before their journey. Since a van driver wasn't available to travel such a long distance at short notice, Charity and Hope had to take the bus, which involved several transfers and nearly sixteen hours on the road, and Caleb knew from experience how grueling the trip would be.

As he deposited eggs into a basket he'd found in the barn, Caleb chuckled to himself, recalling the first morning at the camp when he left the coop door open and the chickens escaped. *At least my boots are broken in now, so I don't have blisters anymore.*

"*Guder mariye*, Caleb." Rose's quiet voice broke through his thoughts.

Turning, Caleb did a double take. Although Amish women sometimes wore their hair down at home in the morning or evening, he'd never seen Rose without hers fastened into a bun and covered with a kerchief or prayer *kapp.* Now her loose tresses softly framed her face and poured past her shoulders in a dark velvety torrent. Caleb couldn't think straight.

"For once I'm wearing a head covering and you aren't," he blurted out.

"What?" Rose's mouth puckered with the word.

"I—I—I…"

Rose tossed her head back and laughed, her hair rippling as she moved. "I think someone needs more sleep. You shouldn't be out here collecting *oier* anyway."

"It's okay. I won't break them. I'm using a basket." Caleb held it up.

"I didn't mean that. I meant I would have done it," she said, coming to his side and reaching into the nesting box. He extended the basket so she could place the egg inside. He might have been quicker picking berries than she was, but her slender hands were more deft when it came to plucking the eggs from the bed of pine shavings. "I was a real shrew to you that first morning, wasn't I?" she reminisced woefully.

"*Neh*, not a shrew. Just a little briary," he teased.

"Briary?" She stopped gathering eggs to narrow her eyes at him.

"*Jah*, you know, like a briar." He took her hand and turned it over to point to where her wrists were embedded with raspberry prickles.

"Oh." She didn't move. Caleb knew he ought to release her fingers now that he'd shown her what he meant, but the best he could do was to loosen his grip. Sadness eclipsed her face. "You're right. I really can get under a person's skin, can't I?"

Jah, *but not in the way you're thinking.* Caleb cleared his throat. "You can't help it—it's all in your name. But a rose is beautiful, too."

As Rose swiftly withdrew her hand to reach into the nesting box again, Caleb thought, *Uh-oh, I shouldn't have said that.* No matter how much he meant it.

Rose wondered whether she should thank Caleb for the compliment. *He didn't actually say* I'm *beautiful—he said a* rose *is beautiful.* He couldn't have been flirting with her, could he? Not here, standing beside the chicken coop first thing in the morning, with her eyes puffy and her hair wild.

Not knowing how else to respond, Rose replied earnestly, "I'm glad you gave me a second chance to prove I'm not always briary. *Lots* of second chances. Your friendship is important to me. Especially now when everything is so—so…" She was overcome with an urge to weep, but she held it in and fastened the coop door shut. "I can take the basket now."

Caleb allowed her to grasp the handle but he didn't let go of his side. When she gave it a tug, he tugged back until she met his eyes. "I'll help you with whatever you need, Rose," he said. "Picking *hembeer* and *blohbier*, checking guests in and out, or—or buying a pair of earplugs so you don't have to listen to Eleanor prattle while you're preparing meals."

Rose chortled. "I don't mind her babbling while we work, as long as her hands are moving as quickly as her mouth is."

Caleb released the basket handle. "Have you thought about how you're going to make extra pies and jam while the *meed* are away?"

"I have a couple ideas. Right now, the most important thing on my mind is making breakfast and sending Hope and Charity off to Ohio."

"Mine, too—after I *millich* the *kuh*." Caleb agreed to come to the dining hall when he was finished. Since the girls were leaving so early, this morning Rose was preparing breakfast for the four of them before making it for the guests.

They ate quickly and then hurried to the barn together. Rose hugged Charity and Hope, and gave them a canvas bag filled with cards for Nancy and Sol, half a dozen jars of blueberry jam to share with their relatives in Ohio and enough snacks to last the girls all the way across the country and back. As she watched the buggy pull away, Rose allowed the tears she'd been fighting all morning to stream freely down her face. *Dear* Gott, *if it's Your will to take Sol home, please at least allow Charity and Hope to get there in time to say goodbye first.*

After praying, Rose sobbed even harder, primarily because she feared for Sol's health, but also because she'd miss her cousins in the coming weeks. Soon she'd have to leave the lake and Serenity Ridge behind; she'd have to bid farewell to Caleb, too. It was enough to make her want to bawl like a baby for the rest of the day, which of course she couldn't. She had guests to serve. Rose blotted her face with her sleeve and smoothed her apron, but as she shuffled back to the dining hall, a few stray tears cooled her cheeks.

"Good morning," a guest greeted her in a hushed voice on the path near cabin four. He carried a fishing pole and his two young children hopped alongside him, one with a pail and the other with a net. They waved happily at Rose.

Glancing up, the man's wife waved, too. "Such a lovely day, isn't it?" she trilled.

"It is, *jah*." Rose forced a smile even though there was nothing lovely about the day. Still, the good thing about having such a long to-do list was that it left no room for wallowing, and by the time Miriam arrived, Rose's eyes were dry and her smile was sincere.

Miriam proved to be every bit as capable and diligent as Charity and Hope. As she punched down the dough for bread, she told Rose she and her mother had visited several houses in the district after Caleb brought her home the previous afternoon. Together they'd arranged coverage for Hope and Charity's babysitting roles.

"Maria Mast can help you and Eleanor prepare and serve supper from Monday through Friday. I'm sorry to say I couldn't get anyone to help with lunch, though."

"*Denki, denki, denki* to you and your *mamm* for recruiting people to help!" Rose sang out. "As for lunch, I just set out bread and cheese, fruit, dessert and paper plates. It's the easiest thing I do all day."

Caleb stopped in later for a second cup of coffee and he seemed almost as happy as Rose was when she told him about the new staff arrangements. "That's what I love about the Amish—everyone's so community-minded."

His comment struck Rose as peculiar. *Community-minded* was how *Englischers* described the Amish in newspaper articles or library books Rose had read, but it wasn't a term she'd ever heard an Amish person use. Serving one another was at the core of their Christian beliefs; it was an expectation, not something to boast about. "Aren't people *community-minded* in your district in Wisconsin?"

Caleb's face felt inflamed. He lifted the cup to his mouth and took a swig to buy time before answering. "*Jah*, they are. I just meant… I meant…" He faltered. "I guess I was trying to say I appreciate the settlement here. The *leit* are especially helpful."

His answer seemed to satisfy Rose. "Speaking of helpful *leit*, is your offer to help with whatever I need still valid?" she asked.

"Absolutely." Caleb took another swallow of coffee; his mouth was so dry.

"Since today is *Muundaag,* I need to deposit the rent. But I noticed the *hembeer* are close to going bad on the north end of the field, so they should be picked this morning—"

"No problem, I'll take care of them. You said the north end, right?"

"*Jah*, but I thought I'd pick the *hembeer* and you could deposit the money."

Caleb balked. "You want me to go to the bank?" Rose didn't even allow the twins to take the rent to the bank.

"*Jah.* Helen is coming soon and I need to talk to her about what kind of pies she wants this week. But if you'd rather not—"

"*Neh.* I'd like to go." Caleb couldn't help teasing, "Are you sure you trust me with all that cash? I might stash it in my *hut* for safekeeping and it could blow away..."

Instead of the smile he'd hoped to evoke, a frown tarnished Rose's expression. "Of course I trust you with the cash. I'd trust you with my *life*, Caleb."

"Denki," he murmured, setting his hat low on his head so she couldn't see his eyes. Caleb couldn't imagine any woman ever saying something that meant as much to him as what Rose had just said and it nearly moved him to tears. Whether that was because he was overcome with joy or overwhelmed with guilt, he couldn't tell for certain.

Rose took an instant liking to Maria Mast. Known for being an excellent cook, she was good-humored, candid and energetic. And, while she didn't initiate idle chitchat herself, she seemed unfazed by Eleanor's incessant jabbering.

"Maria got married last December, didn't you, Maria?" Eleanor addressed both Rose and Maria simultaneously.

"That's right." Maria carried a large bowl of broccoli florets and a colander to the sink.

Now Eleanor turned to Rose, marveling, "She was a first-time bride. She'd never been married and widowed before then."

Recognizing Eleanor was making a thinly veiled reference to Maria being single until she was in her thirties, Rose ignored the younger woman's remark. "Please take the plates into the dining hall, Eleanor," she requested brusquely.

Eleanor scuffed over to the cupboard and removed the plates in twos. "Your husband is from Indiana, isn't he, Maria?"

"Jah," said Maria as she dumped the florets into the colander and turned on the faucet. "I met Otto when he came to Serenity Ridge to visit Levi Swarey, his departed sister's husband. But you were at our *hochzich* and you know this already. Why are you asking me about it now?"

"For Rose's benefit," Eleanor said bluntly, and Rose guffawed at her nerve.

"What would benefit me more is if you'd take those plates into the dining hall."

Eleanor dallied, carefully aligning the patterns as she stacked the tray with dishes. "Did you and Otto have a long-distance courtship, Maria?"

"*Jah*. For a short time, when he returned to Indiana for a few months before moving here permanently."

"That's what I think Rose and Caleb should do once they leave Serenity Ridge. They could continue their court—"

"Eleanor!" Rose was mortified.

Eleanor leaned in Maria's direction and whispered loudly, "She pretends they're not a couple, but they really are."

"That's not true! You know what Scripture says about talebearers," Rose warned, deliberately using a term from the Bible to prick Eleanor's conscience. It didn't work.

"I'm not trying to be a talebearer. I'm trying to point out that there's still hope for you, Rose. If Maria could get married when she was over thirty, there's no reason—"

"Eleanor—the plates!" Rose's voice had a daunting edge to it, so Eleanor finally picked up the tray and retreated from the kitchen. "I'm sorry about that, Maria. Eleanor can be…indiscreet at times."

Maria just laughed. "It's nothing I didn't hear often enough before I got married—sometimes from my own *familye.* They thought I should have married the first suitor to court me. My sister-in-law kept saying I wouldn't be able to have *bobblin* if I didn't hurry up and get married—and that was when I was in my mid-twenties!" Maria patted her burgeoning belly. "But I'm so glad I waited until I met Otto."

Rose had never spoken with anyone except her sisters and mother about marriage, and even they wouldn't have been as forthright as Maria was being about the subject. There was something about her confidence that inspired Rose to confide, "I was planning to get married in Pennsylvania in the upcoming wedding season, but we…we called it off."

Maria turned off the faucet and shook excess water from the colander. "Do you miss having him as your suitor?"

"Neh," Rose answered after a thoughtful pause.

Nodding, Maria wiped her hands on her apron. "*Gut.* As I told my sister-in-law each time I broke up with a suitor, I'd rather stay single my entire life than marry a man whose absence didn't splinter my heart to pieces."

"So would I," Rose agreed.

In the days following the girls' departure, Caleb timed his work in the fields to coincide with Rose's berry picking so he could give her a hand if she needed it—and to his delight, she always needed it. Sometimes they sang as they worked, sometimes they joked and once they prayed aloud for Sol. But Caleb treasured their conversations most of all; Rose truly was like a flower, opening up to him more and more beautifully beneath the summer sun.

On Friday afternoon, she even told him about her recent correspondence with Baker, saying she thought she'd finally made it clear to him they had no future together. This news made Caleb happier than he had a right to be; after all, it wasn't as if *he* and Rose had a future together, either. His heart did a little jig all the same.

"Getting through to my *mamm* might be even more difficult than getting through to Baker. She keeps pressuring me to reconsider a courtship with him," Rose grumbled. "That's one of the reasons I'm not looking forward to going home."

"What are the other reasons?"

"Well, if I earn enough money for the lease—which isn't guaranteed—I'll have to spend most of my time at the café."

Caleb was incredulous. "But running the café is your goal, isn't it?"

"*Jah*, of course it is. But I'll miss working outside, the way I do here. I'll miss the people, too."

"Anyone in particular? Someone whose name begins with the letter *C*, for instance?" Caleb was blatantly joking, but he also wanted her to express she'd miss him so he could say it back to her.

"You mean Charity? *Jah*, I'll definitely miss her. And Hope, Nancy and Sol, as well as Abram, Jaala and Eleanor." Rose was teasing, too, counting on her fingers as she named the people she saw most often. "I'll miss Helen, too."

"Aren't you forgetting someone?"

"*Ach*, you're right!" Rose smacked her forehead. "Henry. Of course I'll miss Henry, but we're going to write to each other every day, so that will ease my loneliness."

Caleb rolled his eyes the way Rose sometimes did, feigning aggravation. "You're hilarious, you know that?"

"Am I? I thought I was *briary*."

"You're hilarious *and* briary."

Rose chucked a blueberry at him but it sailed over his shoulder. "Oops. Guess I *missed you*, Caleb..." She giggled at her own wit. "There. I said it. Are you *hallich* now?"

"Delighted." He tossed a handful of blueberries in her direction but not a single one hit her. "Looks like I missed you more, Rose."

She gave him a saucy smirk. "*Jah*, I know."

Caleb grinned and they resumed picking berries again. He supposed he should have felt guilty for flirting with her when he knew nothing could come of it, but he rationalized it was all in good fun. *Besides, she's flirting with me, too.*

Later, as they were eating supper, Rose mentioned

she'd forgotten to collect the money jar and put the left-over produce away, so Caleb offered to do it for her. When he reached the roadside stand he was alarmed to find the shelves toppled, vegetables and fruit strewn into the road, and broken jars littering the grass. His first thought was a car had accidentally crashed into the small building, but he didn't see any structural damage; nor were there skid marks on the pavement.

Then he noticed Rose's sign, still upright, was thickly splotched with raspberry jam. A big pink blob obscured her name, so instead of reading Rose's Pies the sign now said S Pies. *Spies*. Caleb caught his breath and examined the markings closer. The wide circular smears reminded him of Liam's finger paintings. This was no random accident; it was a message from the thief. It *had* to be. But did it mean the thief believed the Petersheims were spying on him? Was it meant to intimidate them, to keep them quiet?

His mind buzzing, Caleb collected as many shards of glass as he could and set them in one end of the wagon. There was no salvaging the rest of the produce, so he heaped the squished berries and badly bruised vegetables into the wagon and added the money jar to his haul, too. After setting the shelves upright he tucked the defaced sign beneath his arm and carted the whole mess to the barn. Later he'd recycle the glass and chop up the produce for compost; for now, he filled a bucket and grabbed rags, a broom and a flashlight, and returned to the stand. By the time he had finished cleaning the mess, Maria's and Eleanor's buggies were gone, which meant he could discuss the matter with Rose in private.

As usual, he found her in the dining hall preparing ingredients for making pies and bread the next morning.

Caleb hesitated, carefully weighing his words before he spoke. He regretted having to deliver such distressing news when Rose was already burdened, and he hoped she wouldn't fall apart. But when he told her what happened, she just clucked her tongue and shook her head. "I spent so much time making that jam and putting up the produce. I can't believe someone thinks it's funny to ruin it all. What a waste."

"I'm afraid it's not meant to be funny," Caleb said. "I think it's meant to frighten us. It's possible Oliver was right about a criminal being in the area."

Pouring flour into a measuring cup, Rose disagreed, "*Neh.* It's only someone playing a prank—probably the same kids who did this before."

"This happened before?" Caleb struggled to keep his voice down. "When?"

"I don't know, a couple weeks ago."

"Why didn't you tell me?" he yelped.

"Because I didn't want you to overreact, the way you're doing now," Rose said calmly, tapping the bottom of the flour sack. "I don't like what they did any more than you do, but it's not as if someone got hurt or something was stolen. Last time, they even paid for the pie they destroyed."

Caleb was astounded by Rose's naivete. "That's because their intention wasn't to steal money—it was to threaten us. Don't you see? Listen, I know I said I wouldn't go to the police, but now we have no choice—"

"Absatz!" Rose slammed the measuring cup on the counter and flour flew up in a puff. "It was *my* pie and *my* jam that was destroyed. This is *my ant* and *onkel*'s business, and they wouldn't want the police snooping around here. If you can't respect their wishes—especially when

my *onkel* is... When he's...he's *dying*—then maybe you should leave!" Rose fled the room.

Caleb exhaled loudly and rubbed his fingertips hard against his forehead. He never expected Rose would suggest he should leave, and at the moment he was tempted to do just that. But he couldn't abandon her now, when he was more suspicious than ever the thief was in the area. For that same reason, he couldn't abandon his search for the coins. Yet Rose's vehement objection showed Caleb that contacting the police was absolutely out of the question. Which left him with only one option.

He tipped his head to each side to crack his neck before joining Rose in the darkened dining hall. She was sitting at a table, dabbing her eyes with a napkin. He sat on the bench beside her, facing the opposite direction, toward the lake. "You're right. I overreacted. I'm sorry."

Rose sniffed, as if she didn't quite believe him. Or maybe he just thought she didn't quite believe him because he didn't quite mean it. What he *could* say with conviction was, "I have no intention of disrespecting Nancy and Sol's wishes."

"You won't go to the police?" Rose clarified.

"I won't go to the police," he echoed. Bumping his shoulder against hers, he added, "Even though I wholeheartedly believe anyone who'd waste your pie or jam should be locked up in jail."

Rose snickered. "I'm sorry. I overreacted, too. I'm just so—"

She didn't have to complete her sentence for him to know what she meant. She was burdened. About her uncle. Her business. The guests in the cabins. "I know.

But it's going to be okay," he said as much to himself as to her.

For a fleeting moment, she rested her head against his shoulder, and it was all he could do not to press his ear against her head, too. Then she was swinging her legs over the bench and standing up. "I'd better get back to work," she said.

When he returned to his cabin, Caleb considered calling his brother to tell him about Rose's sign, but he decided the news might unnerve him and then Ryan would try to convince Caleb to call the police or to leave Serenity Ridge right away. *I'd better just keep my mouth shut and my eyes open. And from now on, I'll need to stay even closer to Rose.* Which might have been the one good thing to come from someone vandalizing the produce stand.

Chapter Ten

"You have a new sign," Helen observed when she picked up her order on Saturday morning. "Did the pie-throwing vandals wreak havoc again?"

"*Jah.* This time they knocked over the shelves and broke a lot of jars, too, so watch your step. Caleb tried to pick up all the glass, but I've found a few more pieces."

"They ought to be held accountable for what they did!" Helen exclaimed. "Or are you going to justify it by telling me they paid for everything they ruined?"

"*Neh,* not this time." Rose had no idea how she'd make up for the loss. She felt so anxious about the unexpected financial setback that for the first time in her life she seriously considered making the jam on the Sabbath. *I would prepare a supper if I didn't have enough leftovers—what's so different about making jam?* Of course, she knew the difference—supper was a necessity, whereas making jam for financial gain wasn't. Still, the temptation plagued her as she paced the porch Sunday morning, waiting for Caleb, Abram and Jaala to come for worship.

Upon their arrival, Abram and Jaala announced they

wouldn't be staying for lunch the way they usually did. Aquilla King, a widow, had caught the bug that was making the rounds, so they were going to her house to minister to her.

"You look fatigued, Rose," Jaala noticed. "Are you coming down with something, too?"

"*Neh.* I'm just worn-out with all there is to do around here."

"It's a blessing to have Maria and Miriam helping you, isn't it? I remember how grateful Nancy was after you agreed to fill in for her so she could travel to Ohio," Jaala commented.

Rose's face burned; she shouldn't have complained about work, especially because she'd received so much help with it. She was barely able to meet Abram's eyes when he asked if she'd heard from Nancy lately. "*Jah.* She called on Thursday and said Sol is still fighting hard."

"Let's give thanks for that," Abram suggested, and everyone bowed their heads in prayer.

The next thing Rose knew, Jaala was gently nudging her arm. Rose sat upright with a start. Had the men seen her sleeping? She was utterly humiliated by the possibility. As it was, she couldn't imagine what Jaala thought about her.

But when it came time for Jaala and Abram to leave, the older woman embraced Rose. There was no condemnation in her voice as she whispered, "You must get more rest, dear."

The four of them walked out to the porch, where Abram asked Caleb, "Have there been any problems here this week?"

Rose didn't want news of the vandalism getting back

to Nancy and the twins, but if Caleb told the deacon no, he'd be lying. She held her breath, waiting for his reply.

"Nothing we can't manage." Caleb's answer was evasive but true, and Rose could have hugged him for it.

"I'll bring lunch out here," she said after Jaala and Abram left. She ducked into the bathroom to wash her hands and caught her reflection in the mirror. Her prayer *kapp* was askew and there were dark semicircles beneath her eyes. *I* do *look fatigued*, she thought. A nap would do her good—but so would spending the afternoon outdoors with Caleb. She went to suggest they pack a picnic and go canoeing instead of eating lunch on the porch.

"That sounds *wunderbaar.* I was going to suggest it myself, but you seemed tired."

"Why? Because I fell asleep during prayer?"

"Did you? I didn't notice—not until you started snoring anyway."

"I did not!" Rose protested as a tall, stocky *Englisch* man and a skinny *Englisch* teenage boy suddenly came around the corner. She didn't remember them checking in on Saturday.

"Hello," the man said as they climbed the stairs. "Are you the property owners?"

The stranger addressed both Caleb and Rose but he was looking straight at Caleb. *"Jah,"* he answered. Then he clarified, "We're managing the camp."

"My name's Leland Perry. I understand your family experienced something upsetting recently." As the man spoke, the scrawny teenager slouched behind him, picking his thumbnail.

"What?" Caleb was confused. *How did an* Englischer *hear about Sol?*

"Your produce stand was vandalized, wasn't it?"

Caleb's mind spun. Had the man seen the damage in passing? Or was it possible he was an FBI agent or a detective who'd been staking out the property? Then who was the kid?

"Yes," Rose answered succinctly. The *Englisch* word sounded peculiar coming from her.

The man nudged the teenager forward. "Oliver has something to tell you."

The boy's brown hair flopped over his eyes and his hands were jammed into his pockets. Without looking up, he mumbled, "I ruined your pies and knocked the shelves over. Sorry."

That was when it dawned on Caleb that this kid was Oliver *Graham.* The boy who'd been harassing Hope and Charity. Caleb briefly considered telling the little punk if he ever bothered the twins or touched Rose's property again, Caleb would knock *him* over. Instead, he prayed, *Please,* Gott, *help me to show mercy.*

"If you tell us what the ruined items cost, my nephew will compensate you," Leland said.

Your nephew? The man standing before him was Oliver Graham's uncle—the detective. With every fiber of his being, Caleb wanted to pull him aside and grill him about whether anything Oliver had told the girls was true. *I gave Rose my word I wouldn't go to the police—I didn't say I wouldn't talk to them if they came to me.* But Caleb knew that was a weak argument and he couldn't arouse Leland's suspicion by asking questions an Amish man wouldn't ask.

Rose stepped closer to Oliver. "I appreciate your apology and I forgive you. I need to review my book-keeping. Would you and your uncle like a piece of pie while you're waiting?"

Oliver drew his chin back in surprise, but Leland answered, "Thank you, but we're having lunch soon." He turned to Caleb as Rose went into the house. "Oliver said he didn't break any shelves, but you and your wife must have had to clean up a big mess."

Caleb nodded; there was no point telling the detective he wasn't married to Rose.

"Oliver's parents own cottages on Black Bear Lake so he knows how busy the summer season is. Since you spent your valuable time cleaning up after him, he can spend his vacation time helping you with a project here at the camp."

Great! He can clean the stable, harvest potatoes and then mow the lawn by the barn—with a manual push mower. Maybe then he'll have more respect for the Amish. "Repaying Rose will be compensation enough," Caleb answered, as Rose came outside and handed Oliver a slip of paper. He pulled a fistful of money from his pocket and paid her.

"Denki," she said, the only word she'd spoken to him in *Deitsch*.

"It won't happen again, will it, Oliver?" Leland prompted his nephew.

"Uh-uh," Oliver muttered.

"Sure is tranquil around here," his uncle said, surveying the lake before the pair tramped down the steps. "Enjoy your afternoon."

As Caleb watched them disappear around the house, it occurred to him that Leland hadn't said how he'd discovered Oliver was the vandal. *With a detective for an uncle, he probably doesn't get away with much. Al-*

though, someone else might have seen him and told his parents... Then it occurred to Caleb that Rose might think *he'd* reported the vandalism to the police after all.

Before she had a chance to question him about it, Caleb defended himself. "I don't know who told the detective about the produce stand, but it wasn't me."

Rose looked startled. "I know it wasn't. You said you wouldn't go to the police and I believe you."

There it was again. Rose's trust made Caleb feel a hundred feet tall and yet like a complete phony at the same time.

"I don't know *how* Oliver's *onkel* figured out he was the vandal, but I'm glad he did," Rose told him. "Now I won't have to cover the loss for the ruined produce, and you can rest assured that this has nothing to do with any stolen coins."

But that doesn't mean we don't have to be vigilant. The coin thief might still be out there. Caleb didn't want to argue the point, so he said nothing.

"The best part of this is now Oliver can have a clear conscience," Rose added cheerfully. "Baker told me it was terrible knowing he'd done something wrong and could be found out at any minute. He said he wouldn't wish that kind of guilt on anyone."

I know what he meant, Caleb thought. *But sometimes, it's a necessary burden to bear.*

"I'll go change my clothes and stick lunch in the cooler. Meet you by the water, okay?" Rose suggested.

"Are you sure you won't be too tired?"

"Not if you do all the paddling." Rose was teasing, but when they reached the beach, one of the canoes was gone and two guests were setting out in the other one, which meant Rose and Caleb had to use a rowboat. Caleb ended up rowing after all.

"Where to?" he asked. "Paradise Point?"

"That's where that young couple is headed. If it's okay with you, I'd like to go somewhere away from guests. Someplace quiet."

"That leaves the islands or Relaxation Rock."

Or Kissing Cove. The unbidden thought caused Rose to blush. "Relaxation Rock, please."

They were quiet until they reached the other shore, where they climbed the rock and chatted as they enjoyed their picnic. Afterward, Rose reclined on the quilt they'd spread on the flat surface as Caleb devoured a second piece of pie. The sun on her face and the sound of the lake splashing against the sand had a lulling effect and Rose didn't think about her uncle's illness, the guests or earning extra income. Her worries floated away effortlessly, like a leaf on water...

When Rose woke, she bolted upright, embarrassed that Caleb had seen her fall asleep twice in the same day. But he wasn't beside her. She shielded her eyes and scanned the shoreline—he was clambering over the rocks a hundred yards from her. When he noticed her waving, he cupped his hands to his mouth and called, "I'll be right back!"

Rose scooted down the rock on her bottom and waded into the lake up to her shins. "Hunting for a buried treasure?" she asked when Caleb came up beside her. For some reason, the question made him stutter.

"*N-neh.* You were sleeping and, and—"

"Was I snoring again?" she asked teasingly.

"*Neh.* But you were drooling."

Rose nudged him hard enough that he stumbled sideways in the water, catching his balance only by grabbing on to her forearm.

"If I take a dunk, you're going to take one, too!" He tugged her arm playfully, drawing her into deeper water, but she was utterly serious as she pleaded with him.

"*Neh*, please don't pull me out any farther. I don't know how to swim."

Caleb immediately released his grip. "You don't know how to swim?" He sounded astonished.

Rose figured fewer Amish people *could* swim than couldn't. "Don't make fun."

"I'm not making fun. I'm just amazed that you can't swim, yet you have no fear of drown—of being out on the lake."

Rose shrugged. "I never said I have no fear of falling in. But I wear a life vest and I trust *Gott* to keep me safe."

Once again, Caleb was surprised by how Rose demonstrated her faith. He used to think she was reckless—foolish, even—for not being more cautious. But more and more he appreciated how she blended good sense, courage and trust in God's sovereignty. He was still going to watch out for her—that was why he made sure he could see her from where he'd been combing the shoreline—but he realized he might enjoy the rest of his summer more if he worried less.

Rose suggested it was time to go. Apparently, a few of this week's guests had special dietary needs and were preparing their own meals. Rose wanted to be available if they had questions about where to find things in the kitchen. Reluctantly Caleb brought the quilt and cooler down from the rock and loaded them into the rowboat. "Can we circle back the opposite way?"

"You're the captain," she said, giving him a sharp salute.

They took seats facing each other, their knees almost touching. As Caleb rowed, Rose dipped her fingers in the lake and then flicked them dry. Caleb had never noticed the freckles across her nose—or maybe they'd only come out today. When she glanced up and caught him studying her, Caleb smiled and fixed his eyes on a distant hill behind her.

"Two more weeks until the fish fry and canoe race," she reminded him as they approached Kissing Cove.

"And three more weeks until the end of the summer."

"Are you eager to get back to the *kinner*?"

"What *kinner*?"

"The *scholars*. The *kinner* you teach, remember them?"

"Oh!" Caleb pulled so hard on the oars he slipped forward and his knees tapped against Rose's. He stopped rowing but didn't slide back in the seat. His voice was husky when he said, "To be honest, I'm not looking forward to going back to *schul* yet. I don't want summer to end." *I don't want this* moment *to end.*

Rose's golden eyes held his gaze as she leaned slightly—almost imperceptibly—closer to him and nodded as if to show she understood. Or to show she felt the same way. *One kiss. Would it be so wrong for us to share a single kiss?* Caleb knew he couldn't cross that line, but neither could he pull away. He couldn't *look* away. He couldn't even blink. *Help me, Lord*, he desperately prayed. *I don't want to do anything to hurt Rose, but—*

At that second, two people emerged from the woods

about fifty feet from where Caleb and Rose drifted in the rowboat. Caleb gestured toward them with his chin. "Looks like we have company."

Rose bounced abruptly backward in her seat and raised her hand, calling out a greeting. The man and woman looked right at Caleb and Rose, but instead of returning the greeting, they spun around, practically diving back into the woods.

"Was that *Eleanor*?"

"She looked tall enough to be," Caleb replied, hoping he was wrong. He could only imagine the rumors she'd spread about him and Rose sitting so close in the rowboat.

"I wonder why she didn't wave back to me."

"Maybe she was embarrassed to be caught in Kissing Cove with a man." The words were out of Caleb's mouth before he realized how hypocritical they sounded.

The irony apparently flustered Rose, too, because after slapping a mosquito on her shoulder, she said, "I really ought to get back to prepare supper for the guests. Can we cut across the lake instead of circling back in a loop?"

"Sure," Caleb agreed without pointing out today was the Sabbath and the guests had to fix their meals themselves.

Those two catnaps she'd stolen during the day must have refreshed Rose because on Sunday evening she lay awake until almost midnight without so much as yawning. She couldn't stop thinking about how Caleb had almost kissed her—*again!*—that afternoon in the rowboat. This time, she was as sure of it as she was of her own name.

Of course, in the end he *hadn't* acted on his desire, and Rose sensed it wasn't merely because they weren't courting. She even doubted it was the interruption by the couple coming out of the woods. Something else was holding him back from openly expressing his romantic feelings for her, and Rose figured it had to be he thought a long-distance courtship was too impractical. *Considering I'm about to make a long-term business investment and we live almost a thousand miles from each other, he's probably right*, Rose tried to convince herself.

She glanced at the glowing hands of the little clock on her nightstand. It was ten past twelve; one more day of her summer with Caleb was over. She closed her eyes—not to sleep, but to keep herself from crying.

On Monday when Helen arrived to pick up the pies, she surprised Rose by saying, "I heard you were very gracious when Oliver confessed he'd vandalized your produce stand."

Rose squinted at the woman. "How did you know about that? Were you the one who—"

Helen shrugged. "Those of us in Serenity Ridge's hospitality biz are pretty tight. We look out for each other. I might have mentioned what happened to your produce stand to Carol Graham, Oliver's mother. Seems Oliver tracked in raspberries on his shoes and stained their carpet twice this summer. Carol's husband is out of town, so she asked for her brother's help in handling the situation."

Rose giggled. "My *mamm* could always tell where my brothers had been by what they tracked into the house, too."

Helen tapped the side of her nose. "They call it

woman's intuition, but a little observation can go a long way."

"Well, I appreciate your observation and your help. If there's something I can do to return the favor, please let me know."

"Can you stay here year-round and bake dessert for the inn?" Helen asked, causing Rose to chuckle. "Don't laugh—I'm serious. Several people posted comments about your pies online and now the guests ask what's for dessert the moment they arrive. I know you have family and work commitments in Pennsylvania, but I wish you could stay here permanently."

Rose wished it, too. In fact, it was almost all she thought about as the days slipped away. The closer the end of the week drew, the more Rose resented having to work to meet her financial goal. On Friday, as she began measuring ingredients for the next day's baking projects, Rose thought she'd gladly forfeit the café lease for an evening of canoeing or relaxing on the porch with Caleb, instead of having to wait until *Suundaag.*

The cell phone rang, interrupting Rose's moping. *Does someone honestly think we'll have a vacancy this late in the season?* But when she glanced at the display screen, she recognized the Ohio area code. Nancy and the twins wouldn't call on the business phone unless there was an emergency. Her hand shaking, Rose picked up the phone. "*Ant* Nancy?"

"*Jah.* It's me, Rose. I had to call right away to tell you—" A single sob cut Nancy's sentence short.

"It's about *Onkel* Sol, isn't it?" Rose didn't want either of them to have to say the word *died.*

"Jah." Now it sounded as if Nancy was coughing—or laughing. Was she hysterical? Rose hoped the twins

were with her. "The *dokder* said he's turned a corner! My Sol is going to be okay."

Rose gasped. "Praise *Gott*! Oh, praise *Gott*!" she declared, laughing and crying at once, just as Nancy had been doing.

Her aunt gave her more details about Sol's recovery, saying he still had a long way to go and they wouldn't make it back to Serenity Ridge until after Labor Day. Then Rose briefly chatted with Hope and Charity. Afterward, she put away the flour and measuring cups and raced down the path to Caleb's cabin to tell him the good news and invite him up to the porch to celebrate with another piece of pie.

"I like the drawing Liam made for me," Caleb told Ryan when he called him on Saturday evening. He was looking at it as they spoke. It was a picture of two people in an SUV with camping gear and a canoe fastened to the roof rack. Liam had written "Uncle Caleb" and drawn an arrow to the man in the driver's seat, and had labeled the passenger Me.

"Tell him I can't wait to see him."

"Won't be long now. So, any news to report this week?"

"I'm afraid not." When he wasn't taking care of the grounds, cabins and gardens or helping Rose harvest berries and produce, Caleb had been re-searching the woods near the camp in an attempt to uncover something he'd missed earlier in the summer. On Thursday, since it was raining anyway, he'd even broken the staff rules and set out in the canoe after supper to hike the trails near Paradise Point, the one parcel of land he hadn't thoroughly explored yet. But the side trails were poorly marked and he'd spent as much time trying to get his bearings as he did looking for the coins. "I'm sorry I don't have more to show for my efforts, Ryan."

"Are you kidding? Regardless of the outcome, I can't thank you enough for all you've done. It means the world to me, although I understand why you might feel like you've wasted your summer."

"No. This summer has been..." Caleb couldn't say it had been the best summer of his life, knowing it had been the worst summer his brother had ever had. "Summer's not over yet. I'm going to keep searching. And re-searching."

"If you don't find the coins, you don't find them." Ryan sounded uncharacteristically nonchalant. "Either way, it's going to be okay."

Is he in denial? Doesn't he realize he could still go to prison and lose Liam? "How can you be so calm all of a sudden?"

"I guess because I've finally given the situation to God. He's sovereign and I have to trust His plan for me in all of this."

Caleb chuckled. "Rose often says something similar to that."

"Too bad she's Amish. A woman with faith like that is a treasure," Ryan remarked offhandedly. "Anyway, I'd better get Liam ready for bed. Enjoy the rest of your weekend."

"I will." *Just as soon as Rose and I get time alone together.*

Because Nancy and the girls wouldn't be back in time for the fish fry, a group of women, including Miriam, Jaala, Maria, Eleanor and Eleanor's mother, agreed to help Rose organize the event. They were meeting at Miriam's home, since it was centrally located, and Rose had left the camp in Eleanor's buggy right after the women finished doing the supper dishes.

Since Miriam's parents were visiting a sick relative in Unity, Miriam was left in charge of her five younger brothers. Rose offered to spend the night and help her take them to church in the morning. Caleb understood she was reciprocating the help Miriam and her mother had given her, but he still was disappointed. Riding to church with Rose was one of his favorite things to do and now he'd have to go alone. "Guess I better get used to it," he muttered to himself.

As grateful as she was for her neighbors and friends' help planning the fish fry menu and organizing the logistics during Nancy's absence, Rose found herself wishing they'd stop talking about every last detail. She wanted to go to bed. Not that she imagined she'd get much sleep at Miriam's house—her brothers had eaten such large servings of the spice cake Jaala brought they were bound to be awake for hours—but she wanted Sunday to arrive so she could go canoeing with Caleb. It was nearly nine o'clock when they finally wrapped up the meeting. It took the women an additional forty-five minutes to get out the door.

Which turned out to be fifteen minutes less than it took Rose and Miriam to get Miriam's brothers out the door the following morning. *Now I see why Miriam prefers to work in the dining hall over watching the* buwe, Rose thought as the six of them raced across the lawn to take their seats before church began.

After tying a handkerchief into the shape of a rabbit to keep Miriam's youngest brother occupied during the sermon, Rose scanned the room until she located Caleb. He was at the end of the row to her right, sandwiched between Eleanor and Henry. Rose smiled when she noticed he was fidgeting. Was that because he felt trapped, or because he was as anxious for church to end as she was? Rose immediately repented of her irreverent thoughts, but she still wished she could trade places with Eleanor.

After lunch, Rose sneaked away from the kitchen before all the dishes had been dried and put away. She skittered outside to where Caleb was chatting with Henry and Isaiah Gerhart beneath a maple tree. After greeting both men, Rose pointed to a sinister bank of clouds in the western sky. "Looks like a storm is coming. You know how nervous thunder makes the *gaul*, Caleb. We ought to get going." In case Caleb didn't get the hint Rose wanted to leave, she added, "I left all the windows in the dining hall open, too. If we hurry, I can close them before the rain comes in."

"See? Rose agrees with me about the rain. You can't go out on the lake now," Henry said to Caleb. Then he explained to Rose, "I invited him to *kumme* play horseshoes with a group of us men but he said he's going canoeing."

"Ah, well, the rain hasn't actually started yet," Rose backpedaled. As if on cue, a crack of thunder echoed across the valley and raindrops spattered the maple leaves overhead.

"C'mon, Caleb. You can ride with me," Henry offered. "Isaiah can bring the others."

Maybe Rose and Caleb couldn't go canoeing, but they could play a board game or do a jigsaw puzzle on the porch. Feeling as if she and Henry were in a tug-of-war over Caleb, Rose smiled victoriously and asked, "You do know that people get just as wet playing horseshoes in the rain as they do canoeing in the rain, don't you, Henry?"

"*Jah.* True," Henry said thoughtfully. "But if it's raining, *schmaert* people will play horseshoes in the barn. Only a *dummkopf* would try to paddle a canoe in one."

Isaiah cracked up and, to Rose's chagrin, Caleb's lips twitched, too. "Suit yourselves," she said, her cheeks hot. As she turned on her heel to leave, Caleb frowned and mouthed the words *I'm sorry.* It was a small consolation, but at least it showed he regretted not being able to spend the afternoon with her.

On the way home she considered stopping at the phone shanty to call her parents, but she decided against it. Rose was already sad about going home in a few weeks. If her mother tried to push a courtship with Baker on her again, Rose didn't know if she'd be able to hold her tongue—or fight back her tears.

By the time she unhitched the horse and put the buggy in the barn, the squall had already blown over. She wiped rainwater from the dining hall windowsills, and then returned to the main house and slumped into the armchair in the gathering room. *Maybe if I take a nap, when I open my eyes again it will be to see Caleb coming around the side of the* haus.

What she woke to was the sound of the window shade flapping against the panes. Rose glanced at the clock on the bookshelf; it was already four twenty! Caleb must be home by now, she thought as a rumble shook the house. Half a minute later, a torrential downpour pelted the roof and trees and ground. No, it was *hail* Rose saw bouncing off the porch steps. A sequence of flashes lit the air, followed instantly by a deafening crack. *I guess it's a* gut *thing we didn't go canoeing after all*, she admitted to herself.

That didn't mean she wanted to be stuck alone in the house for the rest of the evening. So when the precipitation turned back to rain, and the lightning and thunder subsided, Rose dashed to the cabin to see if Caleb had returned yet. The door was closed, but he didn't answer it when she knocked. Rose noticed rain was blowing sideways through the screen of the big picture window, so she stepped inside to close it. Once she'd unhooked the glass frame from the overhead beams, she swung it carefully forward on its hinge and clicked it shut. Then she retrieved a towel from the bathroom.

While she was mopping up the puddle, Rose noticed a couple of papers the wind must have blown to the floor. She picked them up carefully and as she laid them flat on the dresser to dry, she couldn't help glancing at them. One was a photo of a little boy in *Englisch* clothing and the other was a child's drawing of two figures in a car. They were labeled Me and Uncle Caleb. Caleb was the one driving.

Rose staggered backward and collapsed into the armchair. *There must be a logical explanation for this. There has to be*. She was breathing in tight, rapid gasps, and her heart thrummed audibly. No, that wasn't her heart. Rose listened closer and realized the dresser drawer was vibrating. She opened it and pushed aside a pair of socks to locate Caleb's phone. Rose didn't think twice about reading the text from Ryan, which said: Forgot to tell u last nite u got more mail from univ. Should I send it 2U ASAP? Hope u r taking a Sabbath from yr research. Talk 2U soon. Rose slammed the dresser shut.

Her ears were ringing so hard she didn't know Caleb had come through the door until he asked, "What are you doing in here?"

Rose seized the photo from the dresser top and waved it in front of Caleb's face. "Who is this?" she screeched.

"That's my nephew, Liam. I've told you about him," Caleb replied matter-of-factly. Gently, he took the picture from her fingers and set it on the dresser before slowly turning to face her again. He needed a moment to think of what to say next, but Rose fired another question at him.

"Is he *Englisch*?"

Caleb nodded dumbly. He'd never seen Rose's eyes blaze like that before.

"Are you?"

Caleb sucked in his breath and his eyes welled. He couldn't buy any more time. It was over. He was going to have to say it, the one word that would change everything between them. *"Jah."*

The look on Rose's face could have curdled milk. "Don't you dare speak *Deitsch* to me," she snarled and started for the door. Caleb stepped sideways, blocking her path.

"Rose, please. You don't understand," he implored.

"I understand perfectly. You're not the man I thought you were." She held her stomach and stared off to the side as if the sight of him was making her sick. "I expect you to pack your bags and leave by tomorrow morning or I'll have Abram over here faster than you can take off your *hut*," she threatened, and he didn't doubt she would. He still didn't budge.

"Please, Rose, just give me a chance—"

"No," she refused in *Englisch*, shoving past him.

He reached over her shoulder to press his palm against the door, holding it shut. Yes, he'd deceived Rose, which was undeniable, but she'd forgiven Baker. She'd forgiven Oliver. Yet she wouldn't demonstrate even a smidgen of grace toward Caleb, despite all he'd done for her. Despite everything they'd shared. "If you don't let me explain, then *you're* not the woman I thought you were," he said.

"Let me out of here. *Now*," she demanded, so he dropped his hand. As she stepped through the door, she sneered, "Goodbye, Caleb—or whoever you are."

Which made Caleb so furious if he'd had a pie right then he would have smashed it against the wall.

Chapter Eleven

Rose stomped up to the house, but instead of going inside she paced the porch, nearly as angry with herself as she was with Caleb. That big deceitful liar had been using her the whole time! This was just like what Baker had done. No. It was *worse* than what Baker had done because Baker only lied about money; Caleb lied about who he *was*.

Rose should have seen the evidence that had been right beneath her nose. Caleb's peculiar mannerisms and accent. The way he avoided certain questions and topics. His extensive knowledge of *Englisch* ways. He must have thought he was so clever, tricking her—tricking *all* the Amish people in Serenity Ridge—into believing he was Amish. They'd welcomed him into their homes and church. Into their *lives.* Had he no conscience whatsoever? What was it he hoped to gain by "researching" their community—a promotion at a university? Caleb hadn't struck Rose as someone who was motivated by wealth or prestige, the way some *Englischers* seemed to be. But then, she'd gotten everything else about him wrong, too.

The rain was letting up, but Rose's fury wasn't, so

she strode down the driveway, thinking she should have shoved Caleb into the water when she'd had the opportunity at Relaxation Rock. She reached the end of the dirt road and turned onto the country highway, walking until her dress was soaked through with mist and sweat. Stickier, hotter and angrier than when she started out, she returned to the house and flopped onto the sofa in the gathering room. Rose would have preferred to sit on the porch, but she didn't want to risk seeing Caleb or him seeing her.

I won't have to worry about that after tomorrow, she thought. A new worry took root. What was she going to say when people asked where he was? Despite her threat to go to the deacon if Caleb didn't leave, Rose had no intention of telling the *leit* he was an *Englischer*. She couldn't bear the humiliation of admitting she'd been fooled, and she wanted to spare their feelings, too. She'd have to say he left because of a personal crisis, and leave it at that.

And what would she do for a groundskeeper until Labor Day? Even if Rose had the skill to manage the basic upkeep and make urgent repairs to the cabins, she didn't have the time. She was more determined now than ever to meet her financial goal, and every spare second would be devoted to baking pies and making jam. *I'm not going to let Caleb's behavior destroy my business the way Baker's did.* She decided she'd ask Abram if he'd put out the word she needed help.

As Rose went into the kitchen to make a sandwich, she thought she saw a flash of blue outside the window, but when she looked again nothing was there. *That's Caleb's influence on me.* She snickered. *Turns out* he *was the only intruder who'd ever been prowling around the property!*

* * *

Too steamed to stay cooped up in the little cabin, Caleb figured that, since it was his last day at the camp, he'd search the trails at Paradise Point, for what little good it would do. He'd come to believe the note was a complete ruse, but at least hiking would give him something to do besides stare out his window, stewing. As he climbed the steep incline, he remembered the day he'd suggested racing blindfolded and Rose had gotten so upset when the canoe cracked. He also recalled how peaceful he'd felt watching the fireworks display with her on the Fourth of July. Now she was infuriated with him again. It was as if their relationship had come full circle. He couldn't wait to get out of the loop and go home!

But as he stood at the crest of Paradise Point surveying the wet, green hills and lush valley below, Caleb reflected on the community he'd found in Serenity Ridge. Rose wasn't the only person he'd grown fond of here. What right did she have to push him out? Caleb had an obligation to Sol, and he wasn't going to let Rose stop him from fulfilling it. Not without a fight. So, when he returned to the cabin, instead of packing he decided to take a shower.

He was taking clean clothes from the drawer when he noticed his cell phone was on top of his socks instead of beneath them. It didn't take much to figure out Rose must have read his texts, including the new one from Ryan that said, Hope u r taking a Sabbath from yr research. Caleb plunked himself into the armchair. *Rose probably thinks I'm here to conduct an anthropology experiment*, he brooded. It was one more reason he wanted the chance to explain.

After a few minutes of ruminating, he called his brother and asked him to read aloud the letter from the university. As Caleb suspected, it was a reminder to return his teaching contract or risk losing his fall course load. "Yeah, I guess I'd better take care of that," Caleb admitted.

"Before you go, I have to tell you about something Sheryl and I decided," Ryan said. "We've been praying a lot, and this afternoon we talked to our pastor and officially decided to stop the divorce proceedings."

Caleb was floored. "Are you serious?"

"Yeah. We finally realized it's time to stop fighting with each other and start fighting *for* our marriage." Ryan told him how they'd been going to counseling. They were still working on some issues, but he was moving home the following weekend. "Liam's overjoyed, of course."

Caleb expressed his happiness about the news, too, but after hanging up, he felt so low he crawled into bed even though it was barely dusk. Instead of water against the shore, all he could hear were the sounds of happy families laughing and chatting as they returned from wherever they'd spent the afternoon together. And because it reminded him of what he'd never had, he pulled a pillow over his head and turned toward the wall.

In the morning, Caleb rose extra early to milk the cow and complete his other chores as usual. He brought the milk to the house and knocked on the door, but Rose wouldn't open it until he left, so he set the pail down and went to the dining hall to wait for her inside the kitchen.

She flinched when she saw him leaning against the sink, but as she twirled to exit the room, he announced,

"I have something to say, and I'll follow you around all day if I have to until you listen to me."

Rose stopped in her tracks; instead of facing him, she pulled a bowl from the cupboard. "Go ahead, but you're wasting your breath."

Caleb plunged ahead. "I admit I lied to you about who I was. I lied to everyone here. And on one hand, I'm very, very sorry."

"One hand?" Rose mocked, cracking an egg into a mixing bowl.

"*Jah*—yes, I'm sorry because it was ungodly and deceptive, and I can't even imagine how hurt and angry you must be, but…" Caleb poured out his whole story, speaking as quickly as he could. He expected Rose to meet his eyes or ask him a question or to otherwise show some sign she was listening, but her profile was impassive as she continued baking. By the time he was done, he'd confessed every lie, fib and evasive answer he'd ever told her. He ended by saying, "I know it's asking a lot for you to forgive me, Rose, but I'm begging you to try to understand. You have to believe me when I say I didn't do it to hurt you—I did it to help my brother. And my nephew."

"I understand perfectly." She picked up a wooden spoon and dipped it in the bowl. "Now, please leave the camp."

Rose's abrupt response hurt, but Caleb was prepared for it. *"Neh."*

Rose stopped stirring. "If you leave now, I won't tell anyone about your…*identity*. If you don't leave, I'll go straight to Abram. Everyone in the community will find out. You might not care what the *leit* think of you, but eventually gossip will spread to the *Englischers*. The police will find out you're an impostor, and that won't reflect well on your brother."

Caleb was undeterred. "I committed to working here until the day after Labor Day, and that's what I want to do. And since you owe me a favor, you're going to let me stay."

"I'll do no such—"

"You gave me your word, Rose."

She snorted. "And you think I'll keep my word just because I'm Amish?"

"*Neh.* Because your *onkel* is ill and there's a community event coming up. And because I still want to help *you* meet your goal—"

"Liar!" Rose shrieked, spinning to face him. "You want to stay so you can look for some stupid ancient coins that can't even be used for currency anymore!"

Caleb couldn't blame Rose for distrusting him, but he winced at being called a liar. "*Neh.* I've given up looking for the coins. I want to stay *in spite* of knowing I'm not going to find them."

Rose turned her back to him again. She was stirring frenziedly. Finally she allowed, "If you stay, you are to remain out of my sight. I will not eat with you. I will not talk to you. And you aren't ever to discuss your… your *identity* with anyone else here. Agreed?"

It's as if I'm under the Bann *and I'm not even Amish.*

"Agreed," Caleb said.

On Tuesday, the second evening Caleb didn't show for supper, Eleanor came into the kitchen where Rose was drying the last dish and inquired, "Caleb's not really still outside harvesting potatoes, is he? You two had a lovers' quarrel?"

"Stop saying such things," Rose warned her through gritted teeth. "Or I'll tell everyone you were alone with a man in the woods near Kissing Cove the other day."

"I was *not*," Eleanor protested adamantly before scuttling into the dining hall to help Maria wipe down the tables.

Rose didn't know what, when or where Caleb was eating, but she was glad he kept his word and didn't come to the dining hall at mealtime and avoided her throughout the day, too. She was mostly glad anyway. As the week wore on, there were short-lived moments when her acrimony toward him softened enough so that some small part of her hoped he'd approach her again. She hoped he'd say he was playing a joke that went too far and he really was Amish after all. It was the same kind of wishful thinking that made her long to turn back time to when she still believed he wanted to kiss her…

Then she'd be disgusted with herself for entertaining the thought and even more disgusted with Caleb for toying with her emotions. With God's grace and a lot of prayer, she'd eventually forgive him for that, and for the other ways he'd betrayed her trust. Meanwhile she poured her energy into earning the three hundred dollars she still needed for the lease, while also serving guests at the camp.

The week seemed to last a month but finally Saturday arrived: August 27, the day of the fish fry and canoe race. As Rose waited for Helen to pick up her order near the produce stand, she remembered Jaala suggesting Rose and Caleb should pair up for the canoe race. *I hope she doesn't say anything to him about that this afternoon*, Rose fretted.

"I won't see you again before you leave, but Sally

will be here on Monday morning to collect the order," Helen said after they'd put the pies in her trunk. Rose had forgotten Helen and her husband were going to Europe for three weeks. The *Englischer* gave Rose a small envelope, as well as a hug, and Rose waved until Helen's car disappeared around the bend. Then she hustled back to help Miriam and Eleanor check guests out and clean the cottages.

It seemed the last *Englisch* family had just driven away when the first Amish families rolled up the dirt road. There was a flurry of activity as the women brought food into the dining hall and the men set up charcoal grills outdoors. Because the Unity settlement was also invited, Rose didn't know half of the people in attendance, and she tried to guess which young boy Hope had expressed interest in. *It's too bad the twins can't be here. They were really looking forward to this*, she was thinking as Jaala approached.

"Are you going to join the canoe race?" she asked, just as Rose feared she would. "The last teams to race are taking their places now."

"*Neh.* I need to help fry the fish." The men who were participating in the tournament had been on the lake since the wee hours of the morning and they were starting to come back now. It was their responsibility to clean what they caught and then the women would prepare the fish for frying.

"You've been making meals for guests all summer—let someone else do it for a change. Go join the *schpass*."

Rose didn't want to take part in the race, for fear she'd see Caleb. Since this was a relay, he was helping transport participants to their designated locations on the lake. She figured as long as she stayed near the dining hall they wouldn't cross paths. But Henry had overheard Rose's conversation with Jaala, and he pestered Rose to be his partner until she finally relented.

The teams consisted of four members, with one female and one male racing together in each canoe. Five canoes raced at a time, for a total of twenty participants in the race, and teams wore matching colored arm bands to identify themselves.

The race began at Relaxation Rock. From there, the teams paddled past Kissing Cove and in between the two islands. When they reached the shoreline near the trailhead for Paradise Point, the first pairs of partners would get out and hand off their canoes to their teammates. The second pairs then raced back to the camp, leaving the first group behind to be picked up later.

Isaiah Gerhart used the rowboat to transport Henry and Rose to the area of shoreline below Paradise Point. While they were waiting for Abram to bring the last pair of racers over from the camp, Rose sat on a fallen log beside Henry. Maria and Otto, as well as Levi and Sadie Swarey, were also racing and the four of them perched on the edge of the embankment, dangling their bare feet into the lake. Another young couple Rose didn't recognize—they were likely from Unity—stood off to the side in the shade without talking to anyone else.

"Here comes the fifth team," Maria said, pointing to the water. To Rose's discomfort, Isaiah was ferrying Eleanor and Caleb across the lake.

Once Eleanor came ashore, she taunted Henry and Rose, "I know we can beat at least *one* team here, can't we, Caleb?"

We'll see about that. Irritated, Rose walked over to speak to the couple standing by themselves. Pointing to the small cooler the man gripped in his hand, she remarked lightly, "You brought your own supper? Your team won't take *that* long to get here, will they?"

She'd only been joking, but the man frowned without answering and the blonde woman with him averted her gaze. Rose realized there was something about her that seemed familiar. Rose was about to ask if she was related to someone in Serenity Ridge or if she'd visited their church when Eleanor began to clap and shout.

"Here they *kumme!* I see yellow—that's our team, Caleb!"

"Ours is right behind them. Quick, Rose, get over here." Henry beckoned.

As she and the couple from Unity joined the others on the edge of the embankment, the men began hollering and whistling at the incoming canoes.

Eleanor cupped her hands over her mouth and shouted, "Go, go, go!"

The woman from Unity copied her and the two of them elbowed their way in front of Rose as they vied for position nearest the water. They were both even taller than she was, so Rose had to stand on her tiptoes to see how her teammates were faring. As she peeked over the blonde woman's shoulder, Rose's eyes registered something odd before her mind could process what she was seeing. There was a tiny hole in the woman's ear, as if from a piercing. *I shouldn't judge*, she scolded herself. *I did things on my* rumspringa *I regret now, too.*

There was a commotion as Caleb and Eleanor's teammates got out of the canoe and Caleb and Eleanor got in. Rose and Henry's teammates arrived right behind them, and the blonde woman and her partner's crew came next. Rose's skirt got soaked to her knees as she helped her teammates out of the canoe, but she didn't care. She was so intent on beating Caleb and Eleanor she looped her life vest around her neck but didn't take time to buckle it. "Go, Henry, go!" she urged as she picked up her paddle.

Henry must have wanted to defeat his sister as much as Rose wanted to defeat Caleb, because he paddled with a ferocity Rose didn't know he possessed. Ten strokes later they were within two canoe lengths of catching up.

"We're gaining on them!" Rose exclaimed. Suddenly their canoe was jolted from behind to the right and Rose had to grab on to the side with her free hand to keep her balance. As she and Henry lost momentum, the blonde woman and her partner pulled ahead of them.

"Oops, sorry," the woman said, grinning facetiously as her canoe overtook Rose and Henry's.

Her brilliant smile reminded Rose of diamonds and suddenly she realized why her ears were pierced: she was Julia, the woman who'd requested a tour of the waterfront earlier that season. All at once, everything clicked. *The coins! The cooler! Paradise Point!* Rose's reflexes kicked in and she leaped to her feet.

"Caleb!" she screamed. Eleanor kept paddling, but Caleb gave Rose a backward glance.

"Stop them!" Rose bellowed, frantically waving her paddle as Julia and her partner headed in the direction of Relaxation Rock instead of toward the camp. "They've got the coins. They're going to—"

Before she could complete the thought, Rose toppled sideways, shattering the surface of the water like glass.

Even over his shoulder, Caleb had noticed Rose's life vest wasn't fastened around her chest, but before he could warn her to sit down, she foundered. In one swift motion, he stood, twisted around and discarded his own vest before hurtling himself off the back of the canoe. Caleb cut through the water as if his arms and legs were fins, and he didn't come up for air until he was within twenty feet of Rose. She was thrashing violently with one arm, and with the other she clung to the life vest, which was bunched up beneath her ears. Henry must have dropped his paddle because he was using his arms like oars to row toward Rose. Caleb reached her first.

"Relax. Let the vest do the work," he said. He gripped her by the arm to stop her from flailing. "Here, let's get this buckled—"

It took some wrestling with the straps, but once the vest was properly secured around her torso, Caleb pulled Rose back toward land. By then, the other racing teams had arrived and a couple men waded into the lake up to their chests so they could usher Rose and Caleb the rest of the way in. Eleanor must have fished Henry's paddle out of the water for him because the brother and sister pulled to shore in their canoes a minute later.

"I know you wanted to distract us but jumping overboard was a *lappich* thing to do just to win a race," Eleanor joked, clearly oblivious to what Rose had yelled about the coins.

Caleb waited for Henry to pipe up, but he must not have heard, either, because he busied himself with squeezing water from his pant cuffs without saying a word. *Must have been the shouting from shore drowned out Rose's voice, or else it was because she was facing away from him...*

"I guess I got overly excited," Rose said. "Sorry I frightened everyone."

Was she protecting herself from getting involved, or protecting him from the public humiliation of having his identity exposed? Either way, Caleb was grateful Rose didn't say anything else.

"I think you frightened Caleb the most," Sadie Swarey commented. "He's shaking."

Her husband replied, "He's probably cold. We should get back to the camp so Rose and Caleb can change their clothes."

"There's not enough room for all of us to go at once," Maria pointed out. "I wonder why that other couple took off for Relaxation Rock."

"They weren't from Serenity Ridge so they probably got mixed-up about where they were supposed to go," Rose said, further confirming she had no intention of disclosing Caleb's secret. "They'll *kumme* back when they realize their mistake."

Caleb knew as well as she did if they really were the thieves, the couple wouldn't come back. Most likely, they'd already abandoned the canoe and run through the woods to where they had a car waiting on the main road. By the time Caleb returned to the camp they'd probably be halfway to Canada. While it grieved him to know they were getting away, there was virtually nothing he could do to stop them now, short of involving law enforcement agencies. But the very idea of them disrupting the Amish community's celebration or bringing Rose into the station to tell them what she knew made his stomach turn. Caleb had promised her he wouldn't go to the police and he was going to honor his word. He owed Rose that much; he owed all the *leit* of Serenity Ridge that much.

Gott, *please don't let the thieves get away*, Caleb

prayed simply as Levi ferried him and two other passengers back to the camp. He made the same silent request throughout the evening, which passed in a blur. And after everyone left and he retired to his cabin, Caleb knelt beside his bed and asked again, *Please don't let them get away.*

While he was praying, someone knocked on the door and he opened his eyes, expecting to see a straggler from the fish fry, but it was Rose.

He'd barely stepped outside before she asked, "Did you hear what I shouted before I fell in?"

He nodded. "You told me to stop them. You said they had the coins."

Rose threw her hands in the air. "Then why didn't you go after them? After everything you went through to come here—and after everything *I* went through because you came—you threw it all away? That was just plain *dumm*! You should have chased them, Caleb. Then at least all of your...your *deception* wouldn't have been for nothing!"

In the pause following Rose's tirade, Caleb thought about Ryan saying he and Sheryl had decided to stop fighting each other and start fighting for their marriage. Caleb and Rose weren't married, but they'd had a friendship—a close relationship—that was worth fighting for, too. "I came back because of you, Rose. I was afraid you'd drown." He mustered his courage and added, "I couldn't imagine anything worse."

Rose's lips parted in disbelief. She shook her head. "I had my life vest. I would have been fine."

"It wasn't fastened, so I couldn't be sure of that."

She let her arms go limp at her sides. "Well, *denki* for pulling me to shore."

"*Denki* for trying to help me stop the thieves. You didn't have to do that, either."

"I didn't think it would be fair to your brother if they got away just because I was mad at you." Rose smiled weakly before asking, "Have you called the police?"

"*Neh*. I'm not going to, either."

Rose looked at him askance. "If you expect *me* to go to them—"

"I don't expect you to. I'd *appreciate* it if you went—and so would Ryan—but I respect your decision not to and I trust *Gott* will work the situation out," he told her. "But will you at least tell *me* why you believe they were the thieves?"

A smug smile played at Rose's lips. She described how she'd noticed the woman's ears were pierced and then recognized her as being Julia, posing as an Amish woman. How she'd realized it was likely the same woman they'd seen with a man near Kissing Cove, and the same woman Oliver's friend told the twins he'd spotted in the woods near the camp carrying a shovel. "What else would she be searching and digging for except the coins?"

Caleb was skeptical. "But what makes you think she found them today?"

"The man with her was carrying a cooler."

"It might have been their supper."

"Not likely. They wouldn't have taken off so fast in the other direction if all they were hiding was a ham sandwich." They both chuckled and then Rose said, "Besides, when you consider the Bible verse on the note your brother received, it makes perfect sense the coins were buried at Paradise Point."

"What do you mean?"

"'Lay up for yourselves treasures in heaven,'" Rose quoted the first part of Matthew 6:20. "*Paradise* is another name for heaven. *Paradise* Point… Get it?"

"Wow. I never made that connection." Caleb still had a lot of unanswered questions, especially about who'd sent the note to his brother, but now he was absolutely convinced Rose was right; Julia and her partner had definitely made off with the coins. "Hey, do you think they were the ones who pushed our canoe in the water on the Fourth of July?"

"*Neh.* The waves carried it off."

"Waves? The waves weren't big enough—" Caleb objected before he realized she was teasing him, almost like old times.

Rose sighed. "This was a long day, so I'll let you get some sleep now."

Caleb was tempted to ask if he could accompany her to church one last time but that would be like asking her to pretend she didn't know he was *Englisch.* "Good night," he said instead. "I'll see you…around."

When the full realization of what Caleb had sacrificed for her sank in, Rose pressed her face into her pillow to muffle her sobbing. It wasn't only that he'd let the thieves go in order to pull her from the water that made her weep; it was the hundreds of ways he'd helped her and demonstrated kindness and affection all summer. The thought of being without Caleb in her life was, as Maria had put it, splintering Rose's heart to pieces, and she cried herself to sleep.

The next morning, as she was preparing for church, she found the card Helen had given her on the desk in the hall. She opened it to read: *"Rose, here's a small token of appreciation for making this the sweetest season the inn has ever experienced. Remember my offer—I'm sure our guests would relish your apple, pumpkin and mincemeat pies, too!"* Helen had enclosed five hundred dollars in cash, which was over two hundred dollars more than what Rose needed for the lease, and she was simultaneously filled with gratitude for the gift and grief about returning to Pennsylvania.

As she tucked the money away, a man called her name through the screen door. It was Henry, and his round face was more serious than she'd ever seen it. After she joined him on the porch, he said, "There's something that's been weighing on my heart lately and I can hardly bear it any longer. I need you to listen carefully before you tell me *neh*."

Ach! Is he going to ask to court me? "Okay, I'll try."

"This spring I, uh… I was hunting by Paradise Point and I saw something—someone. I saw two people, a man and a woman, and they were digging—"

Rose gasped. So he *had* heard what she'd yelled about the coins yesterday, even though afterward he'd feigned ignorance. "You know about the thieves, don't you?"

"Jah." He hung his head. "After Eleanor told me about the FBI interviews, I did some research at the library. I felt so bad when I read about the man from the museum being suspended from his job. I wanted to speak up, but I was afraid—I'd already been in trouble with the game warden for hunting after hours. I rationalized that since the FBI didn't question me directly, I didn't need to report what I saw. But I felt so guilty I sent an anonymous note, a clue. I was constantly worried about you and the twins. I kept trying to return to the Point

to see if the coins were there. I figured once they were gone, I wouldn't have to worry anymore."

"Oh! So *that's* why you kept hanging around. I thought it was because..."

"Because I *liked* you? Eleanor may have told you that, but frankly, Rose, you're kind of old for me," he said, which made her giggle. "Besides, I thought Caleb was secretly courting you—until yesterday when you called out to him on the lake, I didn't know he was connected to the coins. He has the same name as the man from the museum—Miller. It's a common name, but... are they related? Is he... Is Caleb *Englisch*?"

Rose nodded, confirming Henry's guess. After the summer she'd had, she was only mildly surprised by what Henry had confided. "I hope you feel better now that you've gotten that off your chest." *I also hope I can convince you not to tell the* leit *that Caleb isn't Amish.* Rose wanted to protect his identity, at least until he left Serenity Ridge.

"A little," he said. "But I think it's time I talk to the law enforcement agencies... And I think, uh—"

"*Jah*, of course. I'll go, too." It was easy for Rose to complete his thought; she'd been thinking the same thing all morning. "You do understand we might get in trouble with the law for not coming forward sooner, right?"

"*Gott* is sovereign. We'll ask for Him to work everything out to His glory and our *gut*."

They agreed to go to the police station together after church. Rose couldn't wait to tell Caleb herself.

Caleb stared out the window, astounded. He'd just gotten off the phone with Ryan, who'd called to report the FBI had apprehended "Julia" and her partner on the other side of Relaxation Rock. Apparently, the agency had been biding its time to catch the two thieves red-handed so prosecutors wouldn't have to rely on the testimonies of reluctant Amish witnesses in court.

"Was she someone you knew at work?"

"Nope. She posed as a temporary cleaning lady. She didn't have a key card but apparently she used mine. That's why the agents thought I was involved. Supposedly she's known to be quite the master of disguise."

I'm not, Caleb thought mournfully after he ended the call with his brother. He was watching sunlight dance on the water, imagining Rose heading to church alone in the buggy, when she appeared at his door. Before he could even cross the tiny room to open it, she was telling him Henry was the person who had sent the anonymous note and that they both intended to go to the police. Caleb shook his head in protest, but Rose insisted.

"It's my turn to help you and your *familye* the way you've helped me and mine."

"That's very thoughtful, but it's not necess—"

"I *want* to do it, Caleb. I should have gone yesterday. I'm so sorry I didn't." Her eyes welled with contrition.

"*Neh*, I mean it's not necessary to do. They caught the thieves on the other side of the lake. Ryan's name has been cleared."

"That's *wunderbaar*!" Rose exclaimed and promptly burst into tears. At first Caleb thought she was overwrought with relief, but when she covered her face with her arm and cried so hard she gasped, it seemed the most natural thing in the world for Caleb to draw her to his chest.

"Rose? What is it?"

"*Gott* forgive me but I can't stand the thought of being without you in my life," she wailed, holding on to him as tightly as she'd clung to the life vest the day before. Or maybe he was the one clinging to her.

"Does that mean you've forgiven me?"

Rose dropped her arms and took two steps back. In the moment before she answered, Caleb wondered whether she could hear his heart imploding. Then she looked him in the eye and said the one word that would change everything between them.

"Jah."

Epilogue

After the wedding service, Abram and Jaala wished Rose and Caleb blessings in their marriage. "I probably shouldn't say this because I don't want to embarrass him," Abram confided, "but I knew Caleb's secrets from the start."

"You knew he was *Englisch*?" Rose wondered why the deacon hadn't warned her.

"*Neh*. I knew he cared deeply for you and the girls. I knew what a hard worker he was and that he desired a stronger relationship with *Gott*."

"He hasn't changed much since then," Rose said, squeezing her husband's hand. "Except for becoming Amish, I mean."

"And I hardly ever forget when to take my *hut* off or put it on anymore," Caleb joked.

After Abram and Jaala went to the dessert table, Nancy and Sol approached. "You're looking strong," Rose said to her uncle.

"Selling you and Caleb the camp was one of the best decisions we ever made. My health is better, I'm closer to the clinic and Nancy is *hallich* to be living near her sisters again. Even the *meed* have adjusted well, especially because they get to *kumme* back here and help you during the summers."

When Nancy and Sol excused themselves, Liam came over and announced, "I like this *hochzich*, *Ant* Rose. And your *haus*."

"Denki," she said. "Who taught you to speak *Deitsch*?"

"*Onkel* Caleb."

"Your accent is even better than his was when he first came here."

Liam looked at Rose with big eyes. "Will people think I'm Amish, too?"

"Neh," Caleb told his nephew. "We'll make sure they know from the start you're *Englisch*. We don't want to trick anyone, do we?"

"*Neh*, but I still need to learn more words so I can talk to the other kids when I come here to go camping in the spring."

"I know someone who can help you with that," Caleb said. He touched Rose's elbow. "I'll be right back. I'm going to introduce him to David and Elizabeth Swarey."

Meanwhile, Rose's mother sidled up beside her. "Such a beautiful smile you're wearing," she said, cupping her daughter's chin in her hand.

"Denki, Mamm," she said. *It's the smile of a woman who has no regrets...*

* * * * *

If you enjoyed this story in Carrie Lighte's
Amish of Serenity Ridge miniseries,
be sure to read these previous books:

Courting the Amish Nanny
The Amish Nurse's Suitor

Available now from Love Inspired!

Find more great reads at
www.LoveInspired.com.

Dear Reader,

If you've ever eaten wild Maine blueberries—the state's official fruit—you know they're smaller, sweeter and often darker blue than cultivated berries. There's evidence to suggest they're more nutritious, too, although *all* blueberries are abundant in antioxidants.

If you've picked them, you're aware wild blueberries grow on shrubs that are lower to the ground than their cultivated or "highbush" cousins. In Maine, wild berries are traditionally harvested manually with rakes to avoid bruising.

And if you've grown them, you've learned that wild blueberry bushes thrive by spreading out over large surface areas of gravelly soil (which, as Rose mentioned, is why her aunt and uncle could only grow cultivated berries on their farm by Serenity Lake).

But I'll let you in on a little secret I discovered about wild Maine blueberries the summer I was writing this book: they taste absolutely amazing with goat cheese on panini. You have *got* to try it!

Blessings,
Carrie Lighte

COMING NEXT MONTH FROM
Love Inspired

Available June 16, 2020

AN AMISH MOTHER'S SECRET PAST
Green Mountain Blessings • by Jo Ann Brown

Widow Rachel Yoder has a secret: she's a military veteran trying to give her children a new life among the Amish. Though she's drawn to bachelor Isaac Kauffman, she knows she can't tell him the truth—or give him her heart. Because Rachel can never be the perfect Plain wife he's looking for...

THE BLACK SHEEP'S SALVATION
by Deb Kastner

A fresh start for Logan Maddox and his son, who has autism, means returning home and getting Judah into the educational program that best serves his needs. The problem? Molly Winslow—the woman he left behind years ago—is the teacher. Might little Judah reunite Logan and Molly for good?

HOME TO HEAL
The Calhoun Cowboys • by Lois Richer

After doctor Zac Calhoun is blinded during an incident on his mission trip, he needs help recuperating...and hiring nurse Abby Armstrong is the best option. But as she falls for the widower and his little twin girls, can she find a way to heal their hearts, as well?

A FATHER'S PROMISE
Bliss, Texas • by Mindy Obenhaus

Stunned to discover he has a child, Wes Bishop isn't sure he's father material. But his adorable daughter needs him, and he can't help feeling drawn to her mother—a woman he's finally getting to know. Can this sudden dad make a promise of forever?

THE COWBOY'S MISSING MEMORY
Hill Country Cowboys • by Shannon Taylor Vannatter

After waking up with a brain injury caused by a bull-riding accident, Clint Rawlins can't remember the past two years. His occupational therapist, Lexie Parker, is determined to help him recover his short-term memory. But keeping their relationship strictly professional may be harder than expected.

HIS DAUGHTER'S PRAYER
by Danielle Thorne

Struggling to keep his antiques store open, single dad Mark Chatham can't turn down his high school sweetheart, Callie Hargrove, when she moves back to town and offers her assistance in the shop. But as she works to save his business, can Callie avoid losing her heart to his little girl...and to Mark?

SPECIAL EXCERPT FROM

HQN

Sarah's long-ago love returns to her Amish community, but is he the man for her, or could her destiny lie elsewhere?

Read on for a sneak preview of The Promise *by Patricia Davids, available June 2020 from HQN Books!*

"Isaac is in the barn. Sarah, you should go say hello."

"Are you sure?" Sarah bit her lower lip and began walking toward the barn. Her pulse raced as butterflies filled her stomach. What would Isaac think of her? Would he be happy to see her again? What should she say? She stepped through the open doorway and paused to let her eyes adjust to the darkness. She spotted him a few feet away. He was on one knee tightening a screw in a stall door. His hat was pushed back on his head. She couldn't see his face. He hadn't heard her come in.

Suddenly she was a giddy sixteen-year-old again about to burst out laughing for the sheer joy of it. She quietly tiptoed up behind him and cupped her hands over his eyes. "Guess who?" she whispered in his ear.

"I have no idea."

The voice wasn't right. Strong hands gripped her wrists and pulled her hands away. His hat fell off as he turned his head to stare up at her. She saw a riot of dark brown curls, not straw-blond hair. She didn't know this man.

A scowl drew his brows together. "I still don't know who you are."

She pulled her hands free and stumbled backward as embarrassment robbed her of speech. The man retrieved his hat and rose to his feet. "I assume you were expecting someone else?"

"I'm sorry," she managed to squeak.

The man in front of her settled his hat on his head. He wasn't as tall as Isaac, but he was a head taller than Sarah. He had rugged good looks, dark eyes and a full mouth, which was turned up at one corner as if a grin was about to break free. "I take it you know my brother Isaac."

He was laughing at her.

The dark-haired stranger folded his arms over his chest. "I'm Levi Raber."

Of course, he would be the annoying older brother. So much for making a good first impression on Isaac's family.

Don't miss
The Promise *by Patricia Davids,*
available now wherever
HQN Books and ebooks are sold.

HQNBooks.com

PHPDEXP0620TP